With This Ring, I Bleed, DEAD!

I0547006

What happens when you lose the love of your
life after the happiest day of your life?

Edited by Charlotte Emma Gledson
& Lyle Perez-Tinics

Rainstorm Press
PO BOX 391038
Anza, Ca 92539
www.RainstormPress.com

ISBN 10 – 1-937758-04-4
ISBN 13 – 978-1-937758-04-2

Library of Congress: 2011944820

Interior design by –
The Mad Formatter
www.TheMadFormatter.com

Cover illustration by April Guadiana

Praise For
With This Ring, I Bleed, DEAD!

"Hauntingly romantic with more than a touch of the macabre, the tales within the pages of *With This Ring, I Bleed, Dead!* will, quite literally, reach in and wrench your heart out."
- Heather Faville www.DoubleShotReviews.com

"The stories in this anthology will make you weep 'til you have no more tears to cry."
- Mandy Tinics, author of *Darkness of Night*

"This short-story collection combines humorous wedding-day disasters with guts, gore, and ghosts. If you like your happily-ever-after served with raw hearts, blood-drenched flowers, and laugh-out-loud insanity, then you'll fall in love with *With This Ring, I Bleed, Dead!*"
- Savannah Kline, author, *Beloved of the Fallen*

Table of Contents

Tarnish

Jay Faulkner

"Can we go now?"

"It's still early, Jessie!"

"… actually, in my mind, it is late," Jessie said, looking at her watch. "I am getting married tomorrow, you know, and tomorrow starts in less than fifteen minutes … I need my beauty sleep!"

"Don't be stupid, Jessie."

"Thanks, Ann." Jessie smiled. "You saying that I don't need it?"

"No," Ann quipped, mischievously. "I'm saying that it is far too late for that. Just be thankful that some clever woman invented the veil!"

"Cheeky tart!" Jessie laughed, aiming a punch at her friend's arm. "Anyway how do you know that it wasn't a man who invented them?"

"Obvious," Ann said, her schoolteacher voice coming out in force. "Had to be a woman so desperate to get hitched that she would hide her face from the unsuspecting victim …sorry, husband, I meant husband!"

"Well then, we should all raise a toast to that very clever …"

"Desperate!"

"… desperately clever woman, who ensured that we can all get married without worrying about how we will look."

Ann, Jessie and the other five girls at the table raised their glasses as they laughed together. The night had gone better than Jessie had hoped for and, despite her concerns she had to admit, that she was

With this Ring, I Bleed, Dead!

enjoying herself.

"You will look beautiful, you know," Ann pointed out, seriously, "and even if you looked like that Ogre from Shrek …"

"His name was Shrek."

"Oh yeah," Ann giggled, the multiple glasses of champagne bringing color to her cheeks, "I knew that. As I was saying, though, even if you looked like Shrek, Carl would still marry you. He loves you!"

"Really?" Jessie joked. "And here was me thinking he was just marrying me for my money!"

"You don't have any money, Jessie!"

"Well then, here's to love!"

Glasses tinkled together as Ann, with a little too much force and too little co-ordination, pushed too hard and champagne and lemonade – the first Ann's, the second Jessie's – splashed out over Jessie's dress. Jumping up she grabbed at a napkin, laughing at the look of horror on her friend's face.

"Don't worry," she smiled, "It's just a dress. Now, if it was tomorrow, and it was anything but 'just' a dress, I would have to fire you as my chief bridesmaid! I'll be back in a minute, I'm going to dry this off."

Leaving Ann in the midst of their friends, Jessie made her way through the throng of people in the dimly lit club and tried to remember where the rest rooms actually were. As she looked around her, trying to see through the press of bodies, she was jostled from behind and nearly fell. A strong grip on her arm halted her fall and, before she realized what was happening, she was whisked back to her feet and came face to face with a brilliant smile; teeth as white as perfect china.

"I'm so sorry about that, it was completely my fault!" A dazzling pair of blue eyes stared at her, into

With This Ring,

her, with such an intensity that she felt herself flush. The man who had bumped into her could have been something out of an advertising campaign. Six feet two, clear tanned skin, eyes that could melt even the hardest heart. Even in a place with so many people she felt that his smile was for her and her alone.

"No, no, it's ok ..." she stammered, and smiled, flustered, despite herself. Clutching the damp material of her dress, holding it away from her body, she looked around.

"Please, let me buy you a drink to apologize," the man said, with another flash of a smile as he looked her up and down, focusing – a little too long – on the portions of Jessie's body that was visible through the damp material. "It's the least I can do. I insist."

"No, really," she said. "I need to find a restroom – I'm wet ..."

"Can I take credit for that?" he asked as he reached out and placed a hand flat against her cheek.

"What?" She stared up at the man, confused and then – her flush growing as she realized what he meant – she slapped his hand away. "Don't be disgusting!"

"Disgusting?" he asked, with a mocking laugh. All humor was now gone from his eyes, to be replaced with arrogance. He looked her up and down, catching sight of the brilliant ring on her finger. "It's just natural, baby, and I can see that you are married so you must have got 'wet' before ...or does your man not do it for you?"

Ignoring his comment Jessie pushed past the man and almost ran through the crowd. Pushing her way through the dancing people, she felt a wave of relief as she saw the restroom just in front of her. Ignoring the 'out of order' sign she walked in, blinking as her eyes

I Bleed, Dead!

adjusting to the flickering light from the broken strip bulb in the ceiling. Standing in front of a sink she turned the faucet on and, wiping down the stained area of her dress, sighed as she realized that she was only making it worse.

"Getting even wetter, I see and I'm pretty sure that isn't for your husband. Are you wet for me?!"

Jessie hadn't heard the door open, hadn't noticed someone else come into the room. The voice – right behind her and so close that she could feel his breath on her neck – was the first warning that she wasn't alone.

It was the only warning.

Her face connected with the cubicle door as she was pushed through it. A hand formed a fist in her hair, knotting it together and holding her head still. She tried to struggle, but she was pushed over the toilet bowl until her whole body slammed into the back wall, she couldn't find any purchase. A scream rose in her throat but as her face slammed into the wall she tasted blood and the scream choked inside her. She felt a hand, smooth and soft like a girl's, reach into her panties and tear them from her. She heard a zip and, with a whimper, she tried to say no, tried to beg him to stop. With a single thrust he ripped his way into her and her voice died with the pain, with the shock, with the realization. Her head and face scraped against the wall with each thrust. He bit her neck, mouthing a babble of obscenities, as he pushed himself deeper into her. With a judder he thrust, then again. Then stopped. He pulled away and she was left, empty, as something trickled down her thigh. Reaching down she felt herself and, wondering why she did it, looked at her hand. She saw the stain of white and red on her

With This Ring,

fingers. The zipper sounded, again, and the cubicle door opened behind her. Without looking, she knew that she was alone.

* * *

The blue lights of the ambulance sent out silhouettes strobing ahead of us, into the emergency room. The automatic glass doors slid closed behind, subduing the screeching, dual-pitched serenade of the vehicle's siren, as a group of women in green scrubs ran to us.

A gaggle, a troop, or is it a squadron? My mind tried to answer the unspoken, inane, question of what a collection of doctors and nurses was actually called. It didn't really matter, obviously, but that was how my mind worked. Put me in a stressful situation and I would try to think my way out of it. Three o'clock in the morning, with my fiancée bleeding out on a stretcher, definitely counted as stressful.

The paramedic's voice came into clear, sharp clarity, as he addressed the gaggle – no, that is geese, definitely geese – of professionals in front of him, handing over a sheet of paper.

"Twenty one year old female, unconscious and unresponsive at scene. Deep lacerations to both wrists, possible arterial tear on left wrist. Pulse weak and thready, heart …"

I looked backwards and forwards between them, like someone in the cheap seats at a tennis match watching an amazing volley, and realized that while their mouths were moving, I couldn't hear the voices. All I could hear, faint behind the barricade of the plastic mask that forced oxygen into lungs that didn't want to respond, was Jessie's breathing.

Shallow and faint.

How is it, one part of my brain, the annoying part that was always asking questions, asked itself, that I can hear her breathing but I can't hear four adults talking right in front of me?

Shock, I answered myself, you are in shock. Not surprising really; it isn't every day that you find your fiancée lying naked in the shower. Even if it were to happen every day, it definitely ISN'T every day that you find her lying naked, in a pool of her own blood, with her wrists open and a razor blade – pristine and above reproach, just the innocent party in the deal – by her side.

"Mr. Dawkins …"

Weird that, I mused, internally, how the blade could look so clean, untarnished, despite the fact that it had just torn through skin, flesh, muscle and possibly even tendons.

"Mr. Dawkins … Carl!"

"… What?" I stared blankly at one of the doctors – or were they nurses? It was so hard to tell. She stared back, a flip chart in one hand as we both scurried to keep up with the stretcher as it was propelled into a side-room. Details began to jump out at me. The short, bitten nails; the loop of keys that jangled in quiet discordance as they bounced on her hip with every step; the color of her eyebrows that didn't match the obviously – and badly – dyed hair. I took in the white tiles, the array of machinery and tools – implements worthy of a horror movie – and then saw the drain. Right below the stretcher as it became still. I barely heard the paramedic count … saw, but didn't see the group of people lift Jessie across from the stretcher to a static bed. I focused on the drain. Jessie's hand – her left one,

With This Ring,

the ring glittering in the harsh white-lights of the re-suscitation area – drop limply off the bed and blood dripped – so quickly … so much! – onto the floor. My stomach lurched as I realized that day after day and week after week, blood spilled into this room, onto this floor and then was washed – flushed like shit – away down the drain.

"Mr. Dawkins, please!"

"What?" I knew that I had already said that, once before, but I couldn't remember when. I was pretty sure that it had been to that nurse – or was it a doctor? They really should wear nametags – but I couldn't re-member why I had asked her that.

"Your wife, Mr. Dawkins, can you tell me what happened?"

I reached out my hand, trying to get between the masses of bodies that were moving – scurrying – around her. Needles were going into skin, tubes into orifices and, all the time, never-ending – thank God, still blood in there, please God, don't let it end – blood was dripping in a constant staccato to the tiles below. Seeing the tremors that caused my hand to jump and shake like a newly caught trout, and realizing that I wasn't able to get close to Jessie – my Jessie – I looked at the woman in front of me, pen held expectantly above the chart, keys now quiet and restful on her hip.

"Jessie?" I giggled, not able to stop it or the bile that rose in my throat as the stench of chemicals mixed with her blood. "She isn't my wife, silly … not until tomorrow."

* * *

"Are you sure that you don't mind me going out,

Carl?"

"Of course I don't, Jessie."

"It's our last night, though."

"We aren't dying you know – at least I don't re-member that being in the vows. You aren't going to bump me off, are you?"

"No! Of course not, silly …well, at least not until after the ceremony."

"Will you wait for the ink to dry?"

"Probably, yes. I mean as long as it isn't one of your old fountain pens. They take forever."

"Well, you simply cannot rush quality you know!"

"I do know – that's why we're waiting, isn't it?"

"Ah – suddenly from the whimsy to the serious, I see."

"A woman is allowed to change her mind, you know!"

"I hope that we are not talking about the wed-ding?"

"Of course not, doofus, you aren't getting rid of me that easily!"

"Until death do us part."

"Now who is so serious?"

"I didn't mean it that way, actually. To be honest a lifetime just isn't going to be enough."

"Well that is why we have eternity."

"Thank God for that."

"I do. Every day."

"Still it isn't too late to cancel, you know."

"…what about the guests, and the reception?"

"Don't be silly. You know I mean the hen night!"

"Well, actually, it is. You are meant to be meeting everyone in less than thirty minutes so, in terms of good manners, 'too late to cancel' was about three hours ago."

"Really? Is there a book about hen night etiquette that I don't know about?"

"Yes. Yes, there is. Not only does it tell you when it is too late to cancel on your friends but tells you how often you have to phone your fiancée to tell him that you love him."

"And just how often is that?"

"Well the book says every sixty four minutes …"

"That is a very precise bit of information!"

"Well it is a very precise book, you know."

"OK. So, you want me to phone you every sixty four minutes, then?"

"No. Don't be silly."

"Silly! Why is it silly to want to phone you every sixty four minutes to tell you that I love you?"

"…because you don't need to tell me. I already know. I have since the day that I first saw you."

"Oho! You knew that I loved you? I thought that love at first sight was meant to tell you that you loved me, not the other way around."

"That didn't happen when I first saw you."

"I am disappointed."

" … I knew I loved you before I even met you. I was just waiting to find you."

"God, Carl, I really do love you!"

"I know, Jessie. I love you too. Now go meet your friends and have fun. You are going to be late, you know."

* * *

"She was late, you know?"

"Sorry?" The nurse – I had figured out, that if she

15

I Bleed, Dead!

had been a doctor she would probably have been elbow deep in blood right now, along with her colleagues – asked, confused. The fact that she was here, talking to me, made me think that she had the time to spare. Then again it could be because I still hadn't answered her original question. I knew that I really should, just as I knew that I really didn't want to.

"For the hen-night," I muttered, pacing up and down as I stared at the medical team swarming around my Jessie like nothing more than a pack of carnivores, scenting blood and moving in for the kill. "Her friends – from work, of course – had told her to be at the restaurant thirty minutes before she needed too. They know her pretty well, you see, she is always late. Even with that little white lie she was still fifteen minutes late. We used to joke that she would be late for her own funer ..."

A sound like a vacuum cleaner interrupted me, thankfully, and I stared as a small tube was thrust into Jessie's throat. Blood was sucked up and out of her small frame, pooling in a container near the business end of the suction pump, as monitors went wild above her head. I didn't need a degree in medicine – which was lucky, mine is in philosophy after all – to make sense of everything on the screen. I had watched enough episodes of E.R. to know that the flatter the lines the worse the situation was. I choked back a sob, swallowing it stillborn before it could give life to hysteria. The lines were almost horizontal.

"There wasn't time for a taxi," I muttered to the nurse, not looking at her. I didn't know which would be worse. The nonchalant and uncaring expression in her eyes as she looked at me – through me – because she had seen this scene play out so many times before

With This Ring,

or the look of concern, of care, of understanding as she tried to reassure me that things would be ok. I didn't know which one would break me so I decided to risk neither.

"I drove her to the Odyssey myself."

"The Odyssey? Over on Belmont?"

"Yeah," I nodded, trying not to stare as a scalpel sliced through Jessie's arm. The wound on her left wrist was widened and, with easier access, one of the doctors performed a trick worthy of Houdini as he seemed to make her hands disappear into the carnage that was once flesh. "We had never been – not our scene, to be honest – but her friends liked it and there is a private area for hen-nights …"

"I meant to ask, actually," she interrupted, softly. Reaching out she took my hand, forcing me – gently and without making it obvious – to turn around to face her. Away from the resuscitation room; away from Jessie. "You are wearing a wedding band already, aren't you?"

The white gold ring sparkled on my finger, a twin of the one that graced Jessie's own finger. I stared at it, silently, and marveled at the juxtaposition of the nurses fingers entwined between my own. So small, so smooth, so warm – so like Jessie's. Reaching out I gently turned the ring on my finger, spinning it around until the engraving on it came into view. Leaning down, her face inches from my hand, the nurse squinted to see the text.

"True Love Waits?"

"It has two meanings, you see." I stated, flatly. Staring over the nurse's head as the ring took up her attention; the message and the small cross engraved beside it holding her rapt. "For me it means, literally,

17

that I waited forever to find her; to find Jessie. All my life I waited, knowing that there was someone out there, someone to fulfill me and make my life complete. Then, two years ago exactly, I met her; I met Jessie. She was outside Church, waiting for her father, and we started talking. From the day on – from that moment on – I knew that my wait was over."

"You said that there were two meanings?"

"Yes," I whispered, watching as the press of bodies around Jessie got tighter, got more agitated. "A more personal wait; a choice, actually."

* * *

"Ann phoned me," Carl said. "She told me that they couldn't find Jessie and that they were getting worried. I tried her cell phone but she wasn't answering so I went over to her apartment. There was no answer so I just let myself in – we have three keys, you know, one for her place, one for my place and one for the new house. We are going to move into it tomorrow – today I suppose – after the wedding and then we will only have one key. That is all we will ever need, she said, the one key to the one home that we will share forever."

"What happened when you got there?" The nurse prompted, gently, as she realized that my voice had dried up. I was staring into the resuscitation room and wondered why it had become so still. Why had it become so quiet?

"I let myself in and heard the water running. She loves the water, you know. That's why we are going to Bali on our honeymoon; the diving there is wonderful this time of the year …"

With This Ring,

"… The water running?"

"Yeah, I knew it was the shower, you see. I called her, from the door, but she didn't answer. I pushed the door open, slightly, and saw her clothes scattered on the floor. The steam in the room made it hard to see anything and, at first, I thought that she had spilled something on her dress. Then I just knew that it wasn't red wine …"

"And?"

"I ran in. She was lying there, at the bottom of the shower, and the water was running red. So red. I thought that she had had an accident …"

"But?"

"Her wrists were open and, I swear this is true, I could see the bone in her left wrist. She is right-handed, you know, which is probably why she could do more damage to the left wrist. She looked at me – right at me …"

"She was conscious?"

"Yes. For a moment. She looked at me and she smiled. Her lips were blue but that didn't matter. She looked so beautiful. She looked at me and reached out; holding her ring. She held my hand – so cold, her hand was so cold, you know – and smiled at me. That is when she asked me …"

"What did she ask you, Carl?"

"She asked me if I could see it …"

"See what?"

"She told me that he had taken it from her, that he had ruined it. All those hours. All the waiting. The choice. And then, in one moment, it was ripped from her! She asked me if I could see the stain; the tarnish. I didn't know if she meant the ring or herself, so I just held her – kissed her – and told her that I couldn't see

I Bleed, Dead!

anything. That she was just my beautiful, perfect Jessie!"

I looked up at the nurse, catching her eye for the first time and my heart broke. She wasn't disinterested; she wasn't just doing her job. She cared, God damn it, she cared! Tears streamed down my cheeks as I opened my hand to show her the twin of the band that encircled my finger. Jessie's ring.

Shining, perfect, eternal.

"True love waits." I whispered, watching as the doctors moved slowly away from Jessie and left her lying there, cold. Alone. "She wanted to wait for her wedding night. She said that God had made us both, intact and whole for each other, and that he made no accidents. She wanted everything to be perfect …"

Falling to my knees I felt something rip inside me and, as the nurse stood there helpless, I screamed. Jessie's ring fell from my hand and rolled to the centre of the room, spinning in place as her blood flowed down the drain.

* * *

The gloomy day grew even darker, a doleful curtain of gray clouds sullenly moving to cover the sky, as the minister brought his eulogy to a close. His deep and resonant voice had clashed with the wordless sobs of the woman to his left and, even worse, the confused jabbering of the small child who clung to her hand as if afraid to ever let go.

There were many other people gathered in the cemetery but it didn't matter to me. I saw them but took no notice. I only had eyes for Jessie's sister and her daughter; almost my niece. Another few months to

With This Ring,

go before her third birthday so, on the day that her aunt was being buried, of course she was afraid, even if she didn't really understand why.

Ten days ago she had kissed her auntie on the lips, leaving a trail of breakfast cereal behind, and smiled as she held her tight and repeated their personal mantra.

"See you later, Alligator."

"In a while, Crocodile."

Jessie's last words to Sophie had been a lie; she never saw her again. Now she never wanted to be alone, not even for a moment. I had made the mistake of kissing her, gently, three days ago while the arrangements were being made. I had told her that I would see her the next day. Her scream had brought Maggie, her mother, running from the kitchen and it had taken nearly an hour to console her; to persuade her that I wasn't going to 'go away' like her auntie – that I wasn't going to die too.

She smiled at me from across the coffin, face wan but full of childish hope and my heart broke. I tried to remain impassive and silent like the tombstones that surrounded us. I wanted nothing more than to reach out across the hole in the ground and ease their pain. I knew that I wouldn't, though; neither reach out nor console them. I had lost my wife-to-be; my best friend; my soul-mate; my reason to be.

I was having enough trouble just remembering to breathe – in, out, in, out – and holding myself together to be of any help to them. All I could do was watch them suffer and envy their tears; if I cried – even just one tear – I knew that it would open the floodgates and I would never stop. I couldn't afford to fall apart.

Not yet.

I still had something to do.

The minister voiced a small prayer, the words passing right through me unheard, before raising his voice in a hymn that I didn't recognize. From beyond the crowd of faces that I knew that I *should* know, but didn't care enough to try, four men moved forwards and gently began to lower the coffin into the ground. Her father, brothers and brother-in-law.

They had asked me. They had tried to persuade me to take my place and help. I couldn't. It wasn't just that I didn't want to put my beautiful, perfect, Jessie into the dark, cold ground. It wasn't just that. It was more, I knew that if I did – if I stood there, on the precipice and watched her descend – then I would want to follow. I *would* follow. I would close my eyes, fall in and lie with her. Forever.

With a low keen, Maggie took an involuntary step toward the dark oak box, Sophie dragged along with her. Stepping around the two nearest pallbearers I reached out to her, grabbing her by the shoulder, and pulled her close to my chest. I held her tightly but, with hands clenched into fists, she held me tighter. As the rain, finally, began to fall in earnest – as if God himself was weeping at the loss of my Jessie – we stood together, as if we were all that the other had left, and I let her sob on me as the ground swallowed my everything.

"It'll be alright," I whispered into her hair. "I promise."

* * *

The Lord is my Shepherd; I shall not want.
The orange glow from the streetlights filtered in through the half closed blinds, sending bars of shadow

across the stained carpet. He knew that, if he took the time, he could probably tell a lifetime of stories from each individual stain. He reached behind him; instead, pulling the cable that folded the blinds closed tightly. He had no time left for stories.

As the gloom swallowed him whole he leant for-wards, reaching into the largest of the drawers that were contained in the bureau desk in front of him. He didn't need to see what he was doing, years of practice gave his hands sight and they gripped the cold glass with ease before placing it on the desk. It was quickly followed by a bottle that sloshed half-full, or half-empty. A spin of the lid, a quick pour of the bottle and an even quicker twist of the wrist and he tasted the familiar burn. Another shot was filled, this one resting in the glass as he twirled it between finger and thumb, the remains of the light catching the amber liquid that sent macabre shadows dancing across the wall. He reached out, lifting a folded wad of paper from the desk and – despite the fact that it was obviously too dark too see – held it in front of him. He had read the words so many times, over the last couple of days, that he didn't need to see them to know what they said; he didn't need to see the images to recognize the faces they showed. They were burned into his retinas. He could see nothing else.

Dropping the paper to the desk he tossed the bitter alcohol into his mouth, holding it there until he needed to breathe before swallowing it down. As the heat traveled through his body he reached into the drawer one last time and closed his hand around cold, hard metal.

He maketh me to lie down in green pastures;

The smell of stale whiskey filled his nostrils as he

I Bleed, Dead!

toyed with the empty bottle. The last drop of liquid rolled at the bottom as he spun the container, slowly, in front of him. He watched the glass shimmer in the remnants of light that filtered into the room, hardly enough to tell the difference between seeing and not. His left hand remained still, cupping the weathered butt of the revolver beneath it.

The weather had turned cold and damp and his shoulders ached as he stretched out his arm across the desk; the heat of the alcohol had been a temporary relief only. He hadn't slept, not properly at least, since that night and the skin across his back felt as if it were being pulled taut with tension. Allowing the bottle to slow to a stop, he reached up and loosened the tie at this throat, popping the top button and sighing as he felt that he could breathe again. For a moment the relief was tangible and he forgot everything else.

Then he looked down. Then he saw the dirt of the grave on his hands and it all came back to him, again.

He leadeth me beside the still waters.

His hand tightened, cartilage stretching audibly as he gripped the gun with enough force to feel the grain in the old wood. He knew each and every mark, knock and dent in it; his daddy had told him the story behind the old ones and, after he had had it passed down to him, he had lived through the newer ones. Had killed through them too.

It had been easy to follow his father's footsteps and join the force. The uniform, the badge, the gun. It had all been a shining beacon to him from the moment that he was old enough to remember. He knew that he never really had a choice; his destiny, his life, was mapped out for him. On the day he graduated from the academy, his father had given him that gun – his gun – and

With This Ring,

the weight of time had been passed along too. Then came that day, three years later, when it had all changed. The day that he had killed the boy. The investigation had cleared him, of course – the kid had been holding up the liquor store and had already shot one person. The shrinks had told him it wasn't his fault – he had just done his job, done his duty. The nightmares told him otherwise. Night after night they whispered to him that he had killed a kid. Fifteen years old. Nothing else mattered.

Three years ago his life had changed. He had quit the force, put the gun away, and had vowed before God to never touch it again.

And he hadn't. Until now.

He restoreth my soul; He leadeth me in the paths of righteousness for His name's sake.

The barrel gleamed, dully, as he lifted it to his face. He could taste the tang of the metal and smell the bitterness of the oil that kept the old girl as fresh as the day she was made. It was a good smell, an honest smell; an old smell. He ran a thumb over the beveled edge of the cylinder, pausing as he suddenly saw the lined face of his father that last time. Cheeks sunken and eyes hollowed as cancer made a lying carcass out of the man he had always been. He had pissed himself, that night, when he breathed his last but at least he had gone out fighting and cursing to the last.

The cylinder spun and he held the gun close to his forehead, listening to the metal whir, clickety-clack, like the cheap roulette wheels in the even cheaper casinos he had sometimes lost his money in – back in the 'good old days'. Before her. Before Jessie.

People had told him that it was the Church, that it was God, that had saved him. In a way he knew that it was true. If he hadn't been so filled with questions that no-one – his family, his friends, the force paid for shrinks – could answer he would never have entered the Church on Fourth Street that he had walked past, blind, day after day. If it hadn't been for the Church – for his struggle to find something, anything, to fill the void in his life, to give him meaning in the chaos – he would never have met Jessie.

And if it hadn't been for Jessie then nothing would have mattered. She gave him meaning. She gave him answers. She gave him Psalm 23 and she gave him a reason to be and a reason to live.

She gave him everything.

She …

Reaching down he gripped the paper, crumpling it as he pulled it toward him. The barrel gleamed, the cylinder spun, and the smell of the past clogged his nostrils as whiskey bile rose in his throat.

It was time.

Yea, though I walk through the valley of the shadow of death, I will fear no evil; for Thou art with me;

The trees shrouded the road, enclosing it and him, in its shadowed grip. The sound of the engine was the only thing that he could hear as he drove through the woods; the road narrow, worsening, as it became little more than an overgrown, rutted track.

He ran a calloused hand over his eyes, blinking back the haze of whiskey fuelled fatigue, and stared at the path of light ahead of him. Twin beams of white pierced the gloom and, at times, he wasn't sure if the lights pulled him along in their wake or if he chose the course.

A light drizzle began to fall in a staccato rhythm

against the windscreen that lulled him with its familiarity. Clackety-clack. Clackety-clack. Clackety-clack. The column of rolled up paper rattled forlornly on the seat beside him while, in the warm, crevasse of his crotch, his father's gun nestled. The wheels hit a bump in the road and the car jumped, and then lurched. The heavy revolver shifted and he felt its weight against his balls. His cock twitched, blood flowing to it and through it, and he reached down to adjust himself. It had been so long since he had felt anything – down there – that, for a moment, he didn't realize what was happening. As he held the gun against himself he got harder, his length pressing against the barrel. The incongruence of the situation – the fact that he would get excited by a piece of metal – brought a giggle into the silence. He didn't try to stop it. He knew he couldn't. He just drove, and laughed, and cried.

Thy rod and Thy staff, they comfort me.

He slowed the car, flicking the lights off, as he turned a corner and pulled up behind the large building. The change from forest to town had passed him by unnoticed. He had simply driven until he got where he knew he had to be. He didn't care how he got there. Light streamed from the second story windows, flooding the area in front of the car with moving shadows, and he squeezed his hardness one last time as he idled to a stop behind the other cars.

He grabbed the paper, slipping it into his pocket where it jostled for prominence with his erection, as he stepped out of the car. The revolver, warmed with his own heat, seemed to appear in his hand of its own volition; an extension of himself.

Turning to the building he walked slowly toward the light.

I Bleed, Dead!

Thou preparest a table before me in the presence of mine enemies; Thou anointest my head with oil; my cup runneth over.

The door flew open, the wind blowing it against the wall with a crash, as rain pelted the carpeted floor with a fury of stinging drops. All movement stopped, all conversation silenced, as nature screamed her way into the room, heralding the approach of the man that brought the others to their feet.

The rolled up newspaper dropped from one hand, fluttering madly in the wind until it landed – face-up – on the floor near the group of people who screamed and jostled. He didn't hear them. He barely saw them. His dark eyes stared at them through them. He stepped into the room, hand on the wooden butt of the revolver at his hip, and slowly closed the door. The furor of noise was muted, but not silenced and he turned to stare at the figure whose face mocked him through the hours of dark and lonely emptiness; a face that was mirrored on the newspaper at his feet that proclaimed that no charges would be brought against the ever-so wealthy man in the alleged rape case. He smiled out in two-dimensional glory, teeth perfect, eyes knowing that he had got away with it. He smiled.

Surely goodness and mercy shall follow me all the days of my life, and I will dwell in the house of the Lord forever.

Carl's eyes tightened as he took in the smile, the eyes that had haunted him. The eyes that had been the last thing that his innocent Jessie had seen before her world had been ripped from her. The teeth that had bitten her neck and the cock that had …

His knuckles whitened as he held the gun tighter.

Gripping it and raising it and pointing it and aim-

With This Ring,

ing it and squeezing it and …

The body – its face, its smile, its eyes now nothing but a mangled memory – dropped to the ground in an explosion of noise and gore. The tension left Carl's body as, through a rainbow haze, he saw Jessie holding out her hands to him.

For him.

He smiled through the heat of the barrel, tasting the gunpowder smoke as it burnt his tongue, smiling for Jessie as his finger tightened and then …

Amen.

I Bleed, Dead!

Repeat Performance

Dorothy Davies

Florabella hesitated in the church doorway, just as she had done a hundred times before. Count them, she thought, one hundred times. This is the one hundredth and first time and still there is no end to the coming here and the going through this and the going home again. I tire of it. I want it to end. It feels as if it will not end. It cannot end until penance is done. How many times, I wonder, does that entail?

She turned and smiled at her father for the one hundredth and first time and they began the slow walk down the aisle. Sunlight through the stained glass windows cast colors before her, petals to walk on, petals that would not catch her satin shoes and cause her to slip.

The church was full of flowers, in huge vases on pedestals, gathered into small bunches on the pew ends, trailing across the altar. Every year they were there, just as the wedding party was there. They too had become trapped in the never-ending cycle. Not a flower was different from the other; one hundred times she had looked at them.

Florabella knew she was beautiful, knew the golden hair cascading down her back would catch the sunlight, just as the silks and satin of her wedding dress would reflect the sun in all its glory. She knew she was perfect, too perfect.

"You look lovely, darling." Her father's words, repeated every time at that moment, causing a pain to pierce her side and into her heart. She only looked

With this Ring, I Bleed, Dead!

good on that day at that time. She knew, as he did, that the other 364 days they lie moldering under the great slabs in the Loverett chapel just over there, where the cameraman was hiding. At least he believed he was. Every year without fail for at least the last ten years, he had tried to capture the wedding, every year he had gone home with a blank film. She gave him full marks for trying.

The guests turned as one at her entrance. Benjamin got to his feet and turned to look at her with open mouthed astonishment, whilst his best man, Jeffrey, was as languid and indifferent to her as always. But then he preferred men, she knew that. Jeffrey was the cause of their problem, the endless repeat of the wedding. Jeffrey, who dabbled in the darkness, had called up demons and helped cast them, the entire wedding party, into this hell.

The vicar, an innocent trapped in their nightmare, stood waiting at the altar. He showed signs of strain, just as he always did. For him, as for all of them, the nightmare was the repetition. They were forced into an exact re-enactment with no chance of breaking the spell. Yet, she knew, if she could find a way to make one tiny thing different, they would go to the spirit realms and carry on a life there. No waking on the 14th July and becoming their living selves again.

She caught a glimpse of utter repulsion in Jeffrey's eyes but saw the usual adoration in Benjamin's. He never seemed to grow tired of seeing his beloved walk toward him, of joining with her in marriage, of going in the landau back to the Loverett mansion and there, there was the chance she had of changing the scenario. Not here, where the wedding went with military precision: hymns, prayers, exchanging of vows, exchanging

With This Ring,

of rings, the heavy scent of the flowers in her nostrils, the sight of her handsome husband in her eyes, the longing for the night in her loins, a night that never happened. She went to the altar - and her grave - a virgin.

Keep your film rolling, cameraman, she thought. It had taken her some time to find out who the person was and what he was trying to do – capture the yearly event on film to prove that ghosts existed. The idea amused her, as did making sure he never caught their images on the mechanical device. It was easy; they were wrapped around in invisibility to all but those with the gift of 'seeing', but film, no. He tried, tried hard, but he would never succeed. And if I have my way, we won't be back next year, she thought with savage intent. Then what will he do for so-called 'Ghost Hunting?' I need to walk away from the vestry after signing my name for the 101st time and say: *Look, silly man, you are on a loser here. We are spirits trapped in a situation we cannot escape. We are not ghosts. In any event, they don't exist. What you think are ghosts are no more than people's lingering images caught in a time loop. Got it? We, on the other hand, are working out a penance for meddling or dabbling or messing with, choose your own descriptive word, with the dark side. That's all.*

But I can't do it, any more than I can change anything that happens when I go through this ceremony every year. With Benjamin at my side, I walk back along the aisle, stepping on the colorful sunshine, smiling at each other, whilst I sense the glowering, menacing presence of Jeffrey right behind us. Each time we do this, each time we re-enact this ceremony, the menace grows stronger. I have to find a way to break this cycle!

Out into the sunshine, the well-wishers gathered outside throwing rice at us, rice which catches in my hair and my bouquet. I shake it out; the birds need it more than I do.

The landau, also is decorated with flowers, awaits us. Benjamin helps me to climb in and then sits down beside me, smiling with contentment and love. It is the best moment of all in this endlessly recycled day. From here on it just goes downhill fast.

"Florabella, I love you." Benjamin takes my hand, the one with its glittering new wedding ring, and kisses it. "I wish this moment could last forever."

"Hush," I tell him, as I do every time. "Be careful what you wish for, you just might get it."

He smiles. Poor darling doesn't understand the powerful thing thoughts and wishes are. Even after all this time.

Loverett Manor is a blaze of flowers and color. A sumptuous feast awaits us. Guests who did not come to the ceremony are standing around, glasses of punch in their hands and, for some, already in their bodies, judging by their red faces and extra loud conversations. We are greeted with congratulations, kisses and handshakes. It is a moment to treasure, especially when you know what is to come.

I sometimes ask myself at this point of the endlessly repeated day, how everyone could be so happy, smiling, confident and forward looking, when they know what is to come. But a thought occurs to me, for the first time, I have to admit. Do they know what is to come? Do we all know what we are doing, or am I the only person who knows that we are reliving this day as a penance for what is to come? I believe I am.

With This Ring,

That is the first change, then. My thinking is different.

It is part way through the afternoon reception, when it begins to go wrong. It is when Jeffrey has consumed enough punch or spirits of some kind to approach me as I am at the large open window, looking out across the lawns at the trimmed hedges and flower beds. He stands by me, breathing alcoholic fumes into my neck. I am aware that despite his tendencies, he has some feeling for me, which has now been taken from him because of my marriage to his best friend.

"You stole Benjamin from me," he begins, as always.

"Benjamin was not yours to begin with."

"Ah, sweet Florabella, that's where you are wrong. Benjamin has always been mine. That which he will seek to put into you he has already put into me."

He seeks to shock me, as if I don't know what homosexual people do with one another to get satisfaction. Little does he know what I have overheard in my time. I am no innocent when it comes to sexual knowledge, only sexual experience.

"I will have him back!" he hisses, so low, only I hear it. And that is when I know I have to act. I turn and throw a curse at him, one I have learned in the dark hours of training as a witch. He falls back, shocked, white faced and unsteady. He leans on a chair and the white slowly changes to a deep dark shocking red.

"Ah, the bride knows more than she lets on. "The hand gestures are something I don't know but the darkness he conjures is real. Guests begin to comment, to cry out, to utter oaths and make for the outside, but too late. The darkness smothers and covers and suddenly the very walls begin to bow outwards, the ceilings to sag toward us and the house – implodes.

No one escapes.

No one.

In the long lonely empty hours I spend in my coffin in my stone sarcophagus, I wonder how I did not realize Jeffrey had been meddling with the dark powers. I was so busy with my own white witch work to ensure I got the man I loved, that I overlooked his work to ensure he kept the man *he* loved.

In the end we all lost, didn't we?

The Loverett chapel was full with so many of us needing to be buried that we were piled on top of one another in sturdy coffins meant to last a lifetime. I am above Benjamin, alongside my parents and a few relatives. I don't like it but at least I get out once a year to re-enact my wedding day, the proudest day of my life.

The cameraman would love to capture the occasion but what is important is the reason why we re-enact this wedding every year. If you meddle with any forces, white or black, there are repercussions. I used my powers wrongly, to try and injure someone. He used his powers wrongly and caused the death of a great many people. Between us, Jeffrey and I committed most of the cardinal sins – and we were condemned to pay the price. Until one or other of us breaks the pattern in some tiny, almost insignificant way, we will be doomed to relive this day forever. He has no intention of changing it. This I know, for he follows the pattern exactly where I hope to put a foot wrong and break it. I see his look, I know what it means.

You helped me create this, you are as doomed to do this as I am.

This I accept, only up to a point. I hoped that my

With This Ring,

change of thinking would change the day this time. It wasn't enough.

I am back in my coffin, back in my dry as dust bones, my wedding dress stored for another twelve months. When the 14th July rolls around for the 102nd time, I will try again.

I wonder if the cameraman will be there next time?

I Bleed, Dead!

Honeymoon

Kristian Gore

"I, Rachel Pickman, take you, James Thurber, to be my husband, faithful companion and my love from this day forward. I give you my solemn vow that I will be by your side when times are good and when times are bad, when you're healthy and when you are sick, when you make me happy and when you make me angry and in times of joy and sorrow. I promise to love you with all of my heart without condition, to support your dreams, to respect you even when you are being silly, for as long as we both shall live."

"And you, James?" the minister said, turning to the groom. James was now scared he would forget the vows he wrote and turned and looked into Rachel's deep brown eyes. Fear left him and suddenly, it didn't matter what he had written, because he wanted to say what he felt.

"I, James Thurber, take you, Rachel Pickman, to be my wife, my partner in life and my true love. I promise to love you more each day and kiss you goodnight every evening. I promise to give you my trust and respect, to laugh with you when you're happy and give you my shoulder when you're sad. I will love you faithfully in good times and in bad, through thick and thin, and whatever obstacles we face, we will face together, hand in hand. I give you my heart from this day forward, for as long as we both shall live."

He felt they were better than the vows he had written, and so did Rachel, who had found them a week before the wedding. The reception was small and lim-

With this Ring, I Bleed, Dead!

ited to just a few friends and family members at the bride's parents' house. Rachel had been with James for several years and was relieved that she wouldn't have to field the questions about when they would finally get married.

It was late afternoon when they left for their honeymoon that her uncle Robert had paid for. It was late spring in Massachusetts, the weather was beautiful, and the limo was taking them to a secluded old family house where her uncle often stayed when he went fishing. They could think of nothing better than to spend their honeymoon surrounded by nature at a beautiful small lake.

It had been a long day and the couple rested in each others arms, still wearing their wedding clothes, as they both held onto the moment. They fell asleep in each other's arms on the winding road and when they arrived at the lake house, they were just in time to see the last of the sunset disappear over the horizon. Rachel sighed and kissed her husband as the driver got their bags into the house. After refusing a tip, the limo drove off leaving the happy couple in seclusion. Off to the side was their SUV which their uncle had driven out for them the day before.

James scooped Rachel up in his arms and carried her into the house that looked completely out of place in the wilderness, almost as if the house had been built with a subdivision in mind. It stood awkwardly by the lake as if it had been torn from a suburban neighborhood and deposited in the wild like a domesticated animal. There was nothing rustic about the house or for that matter, anything special. It was a two storey family home built in the late 1920's by Rachel's great grandfather as part of a failed development deal that was going to turn the area around the lake into an up-scale suburb. The house was in fair shape, despite looking out of place and the pale blue paint was not as faded as it could have been.

"Well, Mrs. Thurber, what do you think we should do with the first few hours of our honeymoon?"

She looked at him with a mischievous smile and wrapped her arms around his neck and kissed him passionately. "Let's get out of these clothes," she said.

"Mmm, that's what I want to hear." He looked at her with a glint in his eye and kissed her.

She pulled away and grabbed one of the smaller bags and headed upstairs to the master bedroom. He followed with another bag. They found the master suite at the end of the upstairs hall and again James carried Rachel across the threshold despite her protest. Once in the room, she started to get undressed and washed the makeup off her face as James started to get the bedroom ready. As he was changing he noticed a note on the dresser across from the bed near the door.

"Rachel," he called into the bathroom. "Your uncle left us a note."

"What does it say?"

"It says, 'congratulations enjoy the house and please help yourselves to the Champagne in the wine cellar.'"

"He has a wine cellar?"

"Yeah, he said wine cellar. Should I go get a bottle and some glasses?"

"You do that and I'll be ready when you get back up here."

He finished changing out of his tux and went downstairs in his undershirt and boxers. He wandered around the first floor until he found the door to the basement in the kitchen. James felt up and down the wall inside the door but could not find a light switch. He checked the drawers and eventually found a flashlight as he heard the pipes rattle from the shower upstairs being turned on. Outside, there was an electric sound he figured was the pump for the well.

Flashlight in hand, he crept down the basement stairs in search of some sort of light switch. The basement was much colder than the rest of the house, the walls were gray cobblestone and the floor was dirt with thick terracotta paving stones that seemed unsteady under his feet. James felt as uncomfortable as a child left in a dark room for the first time. He looked for the Champagne hurriedly but only ended up having to look through again and on the third pass, he found it.

He walked carefully back to the stairs along the unsteady paving stones when he ran into something dangling from the ceiling near the bottom of the steps. James nearly lost his balance and dropped the flashlight which hit the stairs and rolled between one of the gaps as he fumbled with the Champagne. He heard the flashlight hit the ground behind the steps and could see the light on the other side but wasn't sure how to get around to get it.

He set the bottle down carefully on the steps and looked at what he had run into, only to find it was a long thick string that was still swinging. He pulled it and heard the familiar sound of a pull lamp and a dull white light filled the basement. He looked at where the flashlight had landed and started looking around for a way to get at it and finally saw an old push broom in the far corner. James unscrewed the broom handle and went back to the steps and tried to reach the flashlight

With This Ring,

but could not get leverage and gave up.

He pulled the string and picked up the Champagne and went back upstairs. As he turned to shut the basement door, he caught a glimpse of glowing red. He froze and peered into the darkness for a few moments before he finally shut the door, chalking it up to his imagination, sparked by the eeriness of the cold basement. He quickly went upstairs to the master bedroom to find his new bride waiting on the bed in a silky black and blue teddy, her light brown hair still damp from her shower. He set the Champagne down by the nightstand and climbed into bed.

"Are you forgetting something?" she asked, as he started to cozy up to her. "You're freezing, what happened?"

"The basement is freezing, you have no idea. Wait, what do you think I forgot?"

"The Champagne glasses silly."

"Oh damn, I'll run down and get us a couple."

"Hurry back!"

He went back downstairs to the kitchen again and started looking through the cabinets for Champagne flutes but had to settle for wine glasses. He turned with the glasses in hand and stopped. James knew something wasn't right, that something was out of place but he couldn't put his finger on it. Then it hit him. The basement door was cracked open. He was sure he had closed it, but then perhaps not. He crossed the kitchen and closed the door with his free hand and went back upstairs again.

James entered the bedroom and moved to the edge of the bed setting down the glasses and started to open the Champagne. He struggled with it a bit before the cork finally went flying toward the upper half of the

43

window on the other side of the bed. Rachel laughed when she realized what happened.

"Oh shit!" James said as the Champagne overflowed spilling onto the nightstand. He tried to get as much as he could into the glasses before he went over to the window to see if the cork had damaged it.

"How bad is it?" Rachel asked.

"I just cracked it," he said, "I'll have it fixed after we leave."

He went back over to the bed and gave his new bride her glass before he got under the covers.

"So what do you have planned now?" she said in a sultry voice, still lying on top of the covers propped up on one elbow sipping her Champagne.

"Well, it is our wedding night. I know... We can play a game. We each get a request and we go back and forth until we are either satisfied or too exhausted to continue. You make the first request."

She looked thoughtfully at nothing and then said, "You can massage my feet."

"Really, that's all you want?"

"Silly I've been on my feet in heels all day. Besides it's just a start." She winked at him and he got out from under the covers and started to massage her feet.

"Is this good? I'm not doing it too hard?"

"Mmm. That feels much better. I'll let you know when it's your turn."

"Don't fall asleep on me, honey." He said half joking. After a bit she told him it was his turn.

"I guess you could rub my back for a little bit."

"See, now who's starting slow? Refill my glass first."

He refilled her glass and she started to massage his back and then when it was her turn she asked, "What is a fantasy you never told me?"

"That's not part of the game!" James said.

"I don't remember any rules. I tell you what, if you tell me, I'll see about making it happen." She thought better of that after a moment and added, "As long as it just involves the two of us."

"Of course! A fantasy I've had and never told you about? This is so unfair… OK I'll tell you, I always wanted to…"

He was cut off by a loud crash downstairs. They looked at each other and he got up and went over to the suitcase and grabbed a pair of sweatpants and socks.

"Wait here, it's probably nothing but I'll check it out." She nodded at him and he crept out of the room wishing he had a bat or something. He told himself it was probably a raccoon or something that got into the house. He crept down the stairs and winced when one of the steps squeaked under his weight. He crept around the house and turned on the lamp in the living room and saw that another lamp had been knocked over. He looked at it and tried to remember where the lamp had been, then saw it was unplugged. It hadn't fallen; it had been thrown or tossed from the other side of the room. He walked around the downstairs and a nagging fear kept him from checking the kitchen. Finally he had no choice. It was all that was left. He had checked everywhere but the kitchen and cellar. He crept toward the kitchen slowly with his right fist raised and ready. He felt ridiculous, but he couldn't shake the fear. The light from the living room added a dull illumination to the kitchen and he saw something on the kitchen counter. It was some sort of cylinder below the cabinet where he had found the wine glasses, he tried to think what he could have left behind when he was looking for glasses.

As he got closer, he recognized the object and a cold chill went down his spine. He picked up the flashlight and turned it on and looked around the kitchen and saw that the cellar door was open again. Slowly he moved toward the door and slammed it shut. He looked around the room and grabbed a chair from the kitchen table and wedged it in front of the cellar door. He still felt he was being watched as he backed out of the room and then ran up the stairs.

"Get dressed!" he said forcefully as he came back into the bedroom, locking the door behind him.

Rachel stared at him for a moment as he went to the suitcase and grabbed a pair of jeans and a T-shirt.

"What's wrong?"

"We're leaving."

"What? Why?"

"Somebody is in the house and they're messing with us."

"Did you see someone?"

"No. I lost a flashlight earlier when I went to get the Champagne and that noise was someone throwing a lamp and when I checked the kitchen, the flashlight was there and the cellar door keeps opening after I close it." James said frantically.

"Slow down, what are you talking about?"

"I'm sorry." He walked over to her and took a deep breath and calmed himself. "When I was in the cellar, I dropped the flashlight under the stairs, and when I went downstairs it was sitting on the kitchen counter. That noise we heard was from someone throwing a lamp in the living room which tells me someone is in the house and is trying to mess with us. I don't like it, so please get dressed and we'll get the heck out of here."

Rachel went to the bags and got a shirt, jeans and tennis shoes and dressed quickly. They went to the bedroom door and James stopped her and kissed her passionately before he reached for the door knob. He stopped short of the handle, when he heard the squeak from the stairs. He looked at the door and looked at Rachel, putting his finger to his mouth. He looked around the room for something he could use as a weapon. He went to the window but there didn't seem to be a way down and it was too far to jump.

James got down on the floor near the door, hoping he could see the intruder's feet on the carpeted floor. After a few moments he figured the hall was clear, so he unlocked the door and took Rachel's hand and they crept down the hall with the flashlight off, but still in his hand. He crept down the stairs and paused trying to remember which step squeaked in order to try to skip it, but he guessed wrong. The high pitched groan of the step seemed louder than it really was and when he paused again, he thought he heard someone panting from the hall near the front door.

At the bottom of the stairs James directed Rachel toward the back of the house as he anticipated an ambush at the front door. They quietly made their way to the back door and again James stopped dead when he got to the kitchen. Again he saw the cellar door open and the chair he had wedged against it was back at the kitchen table. When he got to the back door, his heart sank as he realized he needed a key to unlock it, even from the inside. He sized up the door and the lock and decided against trying to kick it open. He went to the window over the sink and opened it slowly and quietly.

47

James helped Rachel silently up onto the counter and she slipped through the window and onto the ground. He got up onto the counter as quietly as he could and as he turned to lower himself out of the window, he saw red glowing eyes moving toward him from the darkened kitchen doorway. He could make out a general shape in the dark, but no detail, just the eyes and the hard sound of its feet on the hardwood floor, almost like hooves.

He got to the ground and took Rachel's hand and they started running back through the woods as fast as they could go. He was afraid to look back. He dreaded seeing those glowing red eyes behind him and he urged Rachel to keep up, never letting go of her hand. They raced through the woods away from the house, but not really to any place and Rachel realized this, and wanted to stop. Before she said anything, she looked back and saw in the distance what seemed like glowing red eyes gazing through the darkness and a general shape of something not quite human.

Eventually they had to stop for a moment, still not letting go of each other. They looked back, searching the woods for a hint of what had been chasing them. They sat down together, breathing heavily and holding onto each other for comfort. Rachel looked around and decided they were thoroughly lost. She had only the vaguest idea where the house was but even that was a guess based on the direction they were running and that couldn't be trusted because every time a tree got in the way, she knew they had changed direction a little.

"We're lost," she said, breathlessly.

"The house is that way," he said pointing in a general direction. "And that means the lake should be that

With This Ring,

way as well. If I had thought about it, I would have grabbed the keys to the SUV, but I think if we make it back to the lake, I could get the boat started and we could get to the other side of the lake. I'm sure there has to be another house over there and even if no one is over there, we maybe could get to a phone or something."

"I have my cell," Rachel said, pulling it out of her pocket, "but I'm not getting any signal out here."

"When did you grab that?"

"I grabbed it when I was getting my clothes out of my bags."

"OK, then we just have to get to a place with a good signal."

"James, I'm not sure the house and lake are really in that direction, we did make some slight turns to avoid trees and I don't think we corrected."

"I still think it's in that general direction, besides we really aren't that far away from the house. We can change direction if we need to, if we don't see anything familiar."

"Familiar? I've been here once and you've never been here and it's the middle of the night. We don't even have moonlight to guide us!"

"Don't worry, honey. I have the flashlight."

"What about that thing? Won't it see the flashlight and how do we even know it isn't out there watching us right now?"

"One thing at a time. Let's just try going back the way we came and see how close we can get without the flashlight. At least we have starlight to work with."

She shrugged and they started walking back but after a while, she was certain they were going the wrong way. Rachel wished she knew more about astronomy

I Bleed, Dead!

so she could figure out where they were by the stars, but then, even if she or James did, they didn't know what actual direction the house was in. She couldn't even remember for sure if they were on the east or west bank of the lake but she guessed east, based on where they turned off the interstate.

After a while, they came to an old forgotten grave-yard that must have been a small family graveyard many years ago. James turned on the flashlight and looked at a few headstones and a dilapidated mauso-leum. He brushed dirt from one of the headstones and read the name, "Sylvia Carter." The dates had worn away.

"Do you know where we are?" James asked, look-ing at Rachel.

"I remember hearing that there was an old ceme-tery somewhere behind the house but I didn't know it was this small. I think this means the house is back that way."

"Well then, we will go that way until we see the house and then skirt around it to get to the boat."

They walked for a few moments toward the house when the ground gave way under their feet. James fell awkwardly into the sinkhole and pain shot through his ankle, causing him to cry out in pain. Rachel was able to throw herself to the side and avoid the fall. Light from the flashlight came up from the hole as James started to get his bearings. Rachel carefully looked down into the irregular shaped hole and called down.

"Are you OK?"

"I think so."

"Can you get out?"

"No. I don't think I can put any weight on my left leg. It looks to be about ten feet up but this looks like a

With This Ring,

tunnel."

"Then I'm coming down."

"No, Rachel. You get to the boat."

"I'm not leaving you!"

She started to climb down the sides of the hole when the ground gave way, causing her to slide down onto James's injured leg. He stifled his scream of pain this time and just grunted.

"Now we're both stuck down here." Frustration and anger peppered his voice.

"At least we're together," she said. She leaned over and kissed him. "I think this way leads in the direction of the lake, so we'll either find another way out or hit water or both."

James sighed and put his arm around her and they got to their feet with Rachel holding the flashlight. She helped him hobble down the narrow tunnel that had just enough room for them to walk side by side, dragging their arms along the dirt walls. They made their way down the tunnel toward what they hoped was the lake. The tunnel narrowed a bit more so Rachel went in front, so James could hold onto her shoulder for support. The tunnel became shorter and an opening into a chamber appeared around a corner.

They crawled out of the tunnel onto a hard unsteady surface that looked to Rachel to be terracotta paving stones. The walls of the chamber were gray cobblestone and she wasn't sure where they were. James crawled out behind her and looked around in a terrified wonder.

"I think we're in the cellar," he said. "I don't see the stairs but this is exactly what the cellar looks like, we must be in some room that feeds into it."

"I don't see a door or anything."

"There must be a way in, but more to the point, the other end of the tunnel must lead to some way out as well."

She looked at him quizzically and said, "If this leads into the cellar then we should go back in and get the car keys. Besides, that thing, whatever it is, is probably still outside, which will give us enough time to grab the keys and get out to the car."

They looked for a way into the cellar from whatever room they were in, feeling along the walls for something until Rachel found it. She didn't see it with the flashlight because an optical illusion hid the narrow passage, making them see it as a corner, but when she touched the edge she was able to peer around the corner and see the back of the steps that led to the kitchen.

"Over here!" she whispered to James. They crawled awkwardly around the corner and out from under the stairs. Rachel helped James to his feet and he tested his ankle and winced in pain. He was sure that if it wasn't broken, it was badly sprained. They started toward the stairs and James reached for the thick string to turn on the light and there it was at the top of the stairs.

The creature shielded its eyes from the light and twisted its body away from them. It was feminine in form and had hooves instead of feet but hands much more human like, three fingers and a thumb, all with sharpened thick black nails. It was covered in a light brown downy fur and had a very short tail. Its mouth was excessively wide and canine-like, as were its teeth. As it grew accustom to the light it turned its head toward the couple and the small horns became visible and the glowing red eyes stared down at them. It hunched forward as it navigated quickly down the

With This Ring,

stairs toward the stunned couple. Its face was rubbery and Rachel screamed briefly as its teeth sunk into her throat and crushed her windpipe.

The couple hit the floor with the creature on top of Rachel. Its thick hard claw digging into James's chest as he vainly tried to beat it off of them. The creature reared its head up and tore the flesh from Rachel's neck, hurling it several feet up the steps and then howled. It turned toward James, who still had his arm around his wife. Even as the life drained from her body, it bit deeply into his throat severing his jugular. It started to feast on the couple even before they were completely dead.

Robert Pickman arrived at the lake house a week later in a tow truck. He went in and looked around the whole house accept for the cellar. He cleaned up the broken lamp and then went to a closet in the kitchen and got some cleaning supplies out and added water to a bucket in the kitchen sink. He added a generic solvent to the water and carefully went to the cellar door.

He walked down the stairs with the bucket and turned on the light, revealing what was left of his niece and her husband still holding each other. He started to whistle a country tune he had heard on the radio. He grabbed his niece by the ankles and started to drag her half eaten corpse around the back of the stairs and into the small room behind it. He did the same with her husband. He went back to where he had left the bucket and started to clean the thick terracotta tiles.

He gathered up their things and loaded them into their SUV. He hooked the tow truck up and drove off. He drove down a back road and into a field then unhitched the SUV and drove off down the road again. Eight other cars of various ages dating back as far as the 1930's were in the field with the newer SUV. Written in the back windows of the other vehicles were the words: "Just Married."

With This Ring,

Deception

Jimalyn Lawless

"I don't trust her," said Joan, the wrinkle in her brow deepening. Joan Sims, prided herself on reading people, and most times her intuition was right. Perhaps because this time her son was involved, her feelings were so much stronger.

There was nothing she could actually put her finger on, but she had taken a dislike to Anna the moment they'd met. Perhaps it was something in those icy blue eyes, so cold and unfeeling, almost like there was nothing there. Joan felt a shiver go down her spine at the thought. She stood on the beige carpet of her lounge room, in the large four bedroom house, too large for one person, she had to admit.

Arms folded, feet slightly apart, his six-foot frame towered over his mothers.

Tony wouldn't hear a word said against Anna, he loved her.

"She's beautiful, not just on the outside, but on the inside, where it counts. She's kind, generous, considerate, and most of all, she loves me," he said, springing to her defense. "She's the person I've been looking for all my life, and I'm lucky to have found her. I suppose you're entitled to your opinion," he spat, "but I know she loves me for who I am. You never bought me up to be a snob, mother, and I thought you weren't the kind of person to judge people on their social standing. She may be poor, but she's honest. Anyway, I'm marrying her, end of discussion. It would be nice to have your blessing and support, but we don't need it. I love you, but let me live my own life, and if I make a mistake, which I'm not, it'll be mine and mine alone."

"You know I'm not a snob," Joan protested, frustrated at not getting her feelings across. "I feel she's not right for you, that's all."

His blue eyes grew dark, and flashed with anger as he turned on his heels toward the door, slamming it so hard on his way out, that it shook the paintings and photographs on the wall. These were Joan's pride and joy. When she was younger she would go out with friends, a sketch pad and pencils in hand and her camera, to capture the beauty of the land. She'd sold quite a few. Those on the wall were special; they were portraits of the family all together. Those were simpler days, and they seemed so long ago now.

Outside, Tony leant on the bonnet of his car as the cool night air helped soothe his rage. How dare she call Anna a 'gold-digger!' he thought. I know she's trying to protect me, but I can look after myself! I'm not a child any more. With that thought still resonating in his head he got into the car. Small stones flew as he spun the wheels on the loose gravel, and sped down the driveway.

Joan watched him from the window, and then walked across the room to pick up a photo, framed in silver, from the TV unit. Peering back at her with soft brown eyes beneath bushy eyebrows sprinkled with gray, a turned up nose, that all Tony's uncles had, and yes, Tony had it too; was the face of the man Joan had loved for twenty years. A crop of black hair going gray at the temples, topped this gentle face.

"I wish you were here," she said as she tried to focus on the image that now blurred as a single tear dropped onto the glass. "You were always able to talk some sense into our son."

Joan remembered the night he died, as clear as if it were yesterday. Sitting beside the hospital bed, his hand felt so cold in hers. When she heard the sigh coming from his lips and felt the small squeeze to her hand, she thought he was getting better. Then she heard the machine 'beep' and she knew he was at peace. He had suffered a massive heart attack, and remained in a semi comatose state until the night he died. At thirty-eight he was too young to die.

What am I going to do now? She thought. How can I cope with a teenage son? She remembered too, how she and Tony cried together. He was her strength during that difficult period, and now she felt like she was losing him.

Her hands shook slightly as she filled the kettle and put it on to boil, wiping her tear stained cheeks with her hankie. Tony had never spoken to her like that, never been that angry. A mother's instinct is to protect her child; she couldn't bear to see him hurt. As she sat drinking coffee, she thought about the argument and her statement. She didn't want to admit that maybe she was feeling a little jealous of this young woman, after all, Tony was her only son and she didn't want to lose him. She also had to admit he was right, she should let him live his own life. But she didn't trust that girl. Although she knew she would have to accept Anna eventually, if she wanted to salvage any relationship with Tony.

* * *

They did make a good-looking couple and he was so happy; Anna was radiant in white. Joan did enjoy the

I Bleed, Dead!

wedding despite herself.

Standing at the airport the next day, Tony put his arms around his mother, and kissed the top of her head. "I'm sorry we fought; I know you don't like Anna, mum. I also know you've accepted this situation for my sake."

Joan hugged him tight, feeling tears spring to her eyes. "I do love you son, please, be careful."

"Hey! What's this?" Tony said, holding her at arms length. "We're only going for two weeks. I'll ring and tell you what a great time we're having and how beautiful it is in northern Queensland. If it makes you feel any better, I'll give you the number of the motel we're staying at and if within the next couple of days I don't ring, you can ring me. As for Anna, I'm sure you'll learn to love her, like I do."

Joan doubted that very much and struggled to keep her mouth shut. Just then, Anna joined them and flashed Joan a beautiful smile.

"Don't worry about your son Joan. I'll take good care of him," she said, encircling his neck with both arms. Joan had a sudden image of an anaconda slowly winding around its prey squeezing the life from its hapless body.

The next few days seemed to drag on for Joan. Tony had promised to ring, but to be fair they were on their honeymoon. A few times Joan had to stop herself from dialing the number Tony had given her. She looked for things to keep her busy, things like cleaning out the kitchen cupboards and shopping for items she didn't really need, but found it hard to keep her mind on the task at hand. When a week had past and still no word, her worries grew. She rang the number Tony had given her for the motel.

With This Ring,

Yes, they had made reservations, but no, they hadn't shown up.

"Perhaps," the motel clerk suggested, "they changed their minds about their destination?"

"Tony wouldn't do that without telling me," she said. Her heart sank. What now? She thought. She felt a little silly ringing the police to say her son hadn't rung from his honeymoon, but she knew if Tony said he would ring, that's exactly what he'd do. At first she was dismissed as an overprotective mother.

"A bad feeling in the pit of your stomach isn't exactly evidence," said the gruff voice on the other end of the phone. However he also heard the worry in this women's voice and promised to check on her story. "Leave it to us," the Sergeant said. The police promised to keep her informed of their progress. Nevertheless, Joan couldn't relax; her son was in trouble, she knew it.

Time dragged on, it seemed ages before she got the call from the police saying they had found Tony, and he was in hospital. They didn't divulge many details over the phone and she didn't waste time asking, they could be answered when she arrived. Joan immediately called the airport for a seat on the first available flight to the Whitsunday's.

That afternoon she flew out. Boarding the plane, Joan wondered what on earth could have happened. The police were very allusive on the phone, and had not mentioned Anna. All she knew was they'd found Tony wandering around dazed and disorientated.

She couldn't eat any of the food they offered on the plane, her stomach was in knots. It felt like stepping into a steam bath as she disembarked the plane.

She took a cab straight to the hospital were Tony

I Bleed, Dead!

had been admitted.

"I'm here to see Tony Sims, I'm his mother."

"I have to warn you, he has temporary amnesia, he may not recognize you," the nurse said, with a sympathetic pat on the hand that Joan had placed on the desk. "Please don't stay too long, he needs his rest," she requested after leading Joan to Tony's room. Joan's mouth fell open as she entered. Her previously robust son seemed to have shrunk. The first thing she noticed upon approaching the bed was his complexion. The harsh Queensland sun had left it brown and dried like a piece of leather. Dark cycles surrounded sunken eyes.

Hearing her voice he looked up. The face of an old man greeted her. She found no spark of recognition.

"Hello son," she said, bending down to give him a kiss on the cheek, at the same moment he turned his head away.

"We are cautiously optimistic," said one doctor. "We think he will regain his memory in time. Whatever happened to him was a great shock, and he is dehydrated."

Joan looked at the long tube running down his arm entering the vein at the back of his hand.

Every day Joan came to see him; she would bring some familiar item from her sister's place where, thankfully she could get a bed for as long as she needed it.

Gradually Tony's memory came back, and he was able to tell the police exactly what had happened. Joan listened as she rested her hand in his.

After arriving in Queensland, Anna had suggested they save the price of the motel and camp out.

"But we've made reservations." Tony had pro-

With This Ring,

tested.

"Come on, it'll be romantic, sleeping under the stars. Besides it's too warm to sleep inside, and if it does get a little cool, we can snuggle up and keep each other warm," she had said with a cheeky grin.

"She was very persuasive, I could never resist giving her what she wanted," Tony said, looking at his mother with an apologetic smile on his face. "Anyway, we decided to pitch our tents, and as it was still daylight, we went for a walk. She must have had the whole thing planned out, because she seemed to be steering me in a certain direction. We walked up a big hill and stood admiring the view for a while. In the distance you could see the ocean sparkling like a handful of diamonds that had been scattered across the surface. Further away were hills of indigo blue. They could have been straight out of one of your paintings," he said, giving his mothers hand a little squeeze. "Anna seemed to be getting closer and closer to the edge and I lurched forward to grab her. That's when I lost my footing and slipped. I grabbed onto her arm and for a moment, it looked like she was trying to pull me back. Then, something seemed to snap in her. Her eyes grew dark, her brow furrowed, her hand relaxed in mine and she just let go and I fell. I don't remember much more. I suppose she thought I was dead and being my wife any money would go to her.

"Mum you were right all along, she was a gold-digger, and I'm a fool. I'm sorry I doubted you, can you forgive me?"

"Of course darling," Joan said. "All I ever wanted was for you to be happy, I'm just so grateful you're alive."

The investigation into Anna's whereabouts is on-

I Bleed, Dead!

going.

Wendy

Bruce Turnbull

After the terror, the brutal disfigurement of the large tuxedo man in the cinder lot, the paramedics that were called to Our Lady's Perpetual Sorrow found a girl, not ten years old, screaming her lungs out on the sandstone steps. Her fingers hooked into her skin like claws, pulling her eyes into bloodshot curves. Bystanders told them she was with the Kevecki wedding party (it was the only event scheduled at the church until evening mass– how couldn't she be?). Further investigation among the guests suggested she was in fact the daughter of the man now dead by the white Cadillac, the man folk used to call Andy. The order of events was a little uncertain, and it confused the paramedics a great deal. Andy Kevecki's wife-to-be was nowhere to be found, and the murder weapon had also gone AWOL (though there were people who knew what had happened, and could describe it clearly). It seemed, however, if they were going to get to the truth of the matter, they had to speak with the girl, who was currently in the wild throes of hysteria.

The paramedics (just two by this point, with more on the way) took her to an ambulance at the rear of the lot, its chrome fender blinking in the high summer sun. They fixed her with an oxygen mask to calm her down. After a moment, her body ceased its convulsions, the crowd dispersed at the church, and as cruisers brandishing the symbol of the Nassau County Police Department rolled into the lot, the girl (who told them her name was Wendy) opened up about the incident and how it came to be.

All agreed it was ghastly business.

It started one night in March. Andy Kevecki had picked his daughter up from soccer practice, the only sport she went out for, with Katy Perry or some other pop slut licking the radio speakers from behind the DJ's iTunes playlist. Andy had just come from the restaurant. It had been his now for almost two years and even in the recession, business was booming. He supposed it had something to do with his menu; it was low-priced and affordable, a complimentary mix of Italian and American. It wasn't the most original place a guy and his family could grab a meal, but it held sway over much of Easterbury, the small suburb within Oyster Bay, where they lived.

People got tired of the same old seafood, especially this close to the Long Island Sound. Even folk from the plush neighborhoods of Cove Neck and Centre Island came out to visit Kevecki's. It had a good reputation. So did Andy. It formed one of the bonds between him and his daughter, who loved his cooking, and would always look forward to meal times with her father (*he's a big, doughy teddy-bear*, she used to think, before she got too old to love him that way). Andy's wife, Catherine, had been good for Wendy when she was still around. It was unfortunate that she only spent two years with her daughter before she complained of headaches, forgetfulness, and horrid nightmares that crawled over her in bed like poisonous spiders. When she collapsed while serving customers at a deli in Brookville (where Andy also worked at the time) Andy's mind went straight to the possibility that all of this was connected, and sure enough, when he got to the emergency room, his fears found a foothold.

With This Ring,

He could still remember the way the words bounced around his skull, like a jack-in-a-box free of restraint: *subdural hematoma, Andy! She had a brain hemorrhage! That means stab, stab, ka-boom, splat!*

Wendy wasn't old enough to understand the gravity of her passing. When she started kindergarten, she often came home and asked why she didn't have a mommy. (It had been apparent before that, but Andy had a way of explaining to her that even though Catherine left, it wasn't her fault and she shouldn't feel bad). There had been other women, of course, but fleeting romances, nothing more. Andy carried a lot of weight with him (some smart-ass at the restaurant joked that he ate his mistakes). He knew if he slimmed down he'd have a lot of game, but it didn't bother him. He had enough to take care of, what with Wendy and her problems.

The rain had come steadily over the past week. Storms like those that whipped through summer, drenched much of Nassau County, slicking the sand in the Bay Cove, bringing the Cold Spring Harbor ever closer to the approaching land. Down on East Main, as he sped toward the Bay, Andy saw the hulked shadow of a Lexus just off the asphalt, with two wheels perched above the sinking mud, like a tightrope walker about to go over. He wrinkled his brow as they passed. Wendy was in the backseat, playing with her dolls. She was maybe too old to be doing that, but Andy didn't mind. Whatever kept her out of mischief was good for his heart.

And yet, the closer they got to the turn for Pine Hollow, and so, to the tree-lined road into Easterbury, the more Andy thought about the Lexus and how it lay there, like a squashed insect, in the glittering gloom. It had to belong to somebody. *Maybe someone out here*, he thought, *on the cool blacktop.*

Just as he considered going back to wait for the owner, he caught movement in the rearview mirror. It was slight at first, just a hint of something black, shuffling in the corner of his vision, but once he knew to look for it, it was there in all its splendor, a wounded animal, perhaps, a coyote from some distant park. Andy hit the brakes and his Beemer came to a stop. Wendy looked up from her dolls, disrupted by the immediacy of their standstill.

"What's wrong, Dad?"

Andy's eyes went to the rearview. "There's someone back there."

Wendy craned her neck, saw it, and turned back.

"Dangerous," was all she said.

Andy put the BMW in reverse and started backing up. He felt Wendy's panic as she flung the Barbie to the floor, twisting her seatbelt until it gobbled her like a leather tongue, thrashing back and forth between the window and her father.

"Dad, let's go! They could have a knife or something!"

Under the sound of spinning wheels, he said, "Wendy, I know what I'm doing. You just sit tight now."

She closed her eyes and went back to what Dr. Weinstein said, way back in December (*next time you feel like getting mad with someone, remember a happy memory – concentrate, Wendy: what is your happiest memory?*), and she thought of the bunny rabbit and the boys behind Hyde Hills Junior High, the ones who hung out in the park with loud, sparkling surprises (*just watch it go, girl, you'll be amazed! Light fuse, run*

With This Ring.

like hell, ha-ha!).

By the time she opened her eyes, Andy had already pulled the car up to the walking shadow, who by this point had revealed herself to be a young woman in an oversized denim jacket, with a brown leather purse slung over one shoulder. Andy hit the horn even though they were the only car on the road. The woman stopped, wide-eyed, and slowly made her way to the BMW. Immediately, Wendy felt a thirst for blood. She hated this woman, this fragile-looking creature, out here in the gathering darkness, alone and vulnerable (*you'd like to tie her to a rocket and send her to the moon, oh, wouldn't that be sweet?*) Andy powered down the window and she came forward, leaning in like the hookers Wendy had seen on TV. Andy got all smiley and that enraged her even more. He was a sucker for those in need.

"That your Lexus back there?" he asked the woman.

She waved toward the spot where they'd seen the car, carelessly, as if she'd forgotten it was there.

"I ran out of gas," she said. "Then this rain..."

The clouds overhead were of the thick, grumbling kind. The rain had stopped temporarily, but Andy knew it would be back (Wendy hoped not – *it puts fires out*).

"Where are you heading?" Andy asked.

"I got a place in Sea Cliff. You know, I was just heading into Easterbury to call a tow truck. No cell signal around here."

"I'm going to Easterbury myself. Hop in."

"No, that's okay."

"Come on. It's no trouble. I'll give you a ride."

The woman seemed to consider this, getting in a

67

car with a stranger, but then her eyes went to the little blond thing in the backseat, to the dolls that lay almost disfigured against the upholstery. It seemed to calm her.

"You twisted my arm," she said, and as she opened the door, a peal of thunder cracked the heavens, and Wendy felt a blade of ice enter her stomach.

In front of the headlights, the woods got lost in a gray sheet. Rain thumped against the windshield, like birds falling from the sky.

"I'm Kerri," the woman said, and shook Andy's hand.

"Andy," he said. "This here is Wendy."

The woman named Kerri turned around, smiled at Wendy, and gave her a little finger-wave that she felt tinkling up her spine, accompanied by a sound in her head of a store-bell jingling. They pulled away from the spot near the woods and followed the unfolding road toward Easterbury. In the silence, Andy and Kerri got to talking.

"You know, I'm pretty glad you stopped for me. You see a Beemer out there, you don't think the guy's gonna give you a hand."

"What do you mean?"

"Well, no offense, it's just this is obviously a new model. These things don't come cheap. Men who drive expensive cars aren't usually the chivalrous type."

"You know BMWs?"

Kerri shrugged. "My dad owned an auto shop when I was a kid. I grew up under the hood."

This brought a smile to his face. "I used to own a Chevy convertible."

"Get out!"

"It's true. I sold it at a great price."

With This Ring,

"How come?"

Andy's eyes went to the rearview, to his daughter. "It wasn't all that good for transporting cargo."

"I can hear you, Dad."

Kerri laughed. "She's a cool customer, isn't she?"

"Boy howdy. Just don't set up a meeting between her and some bottle rockets. Not unless you plan on adding an eye patch to your future wardrobe."

They pulled up at a gas station outside East Norwich. The rain here was lashing against the sidewalk. When Kerri went inside to use the payphone, Andy turned to Wendy, his eyes sparkling in the luminous gas pumps.

"Kerri's real friendly, don't cha think?"

"I guess."

He sensed her trepidation. "What's wrong?"

Wendy pulled at the hair of one of her dolls. The way the rain made the Texaco sign flicker made her think of the rabbit, the explosion.

"She's too young for you," she said.

Andy looked shocked. "You think she's interested in me?"

"What, with her 'Oh, a nice guy who drives a fancy car ain't gonna stop for a little princess like me' routine? Yeah, Dad. She's way into you."

"You really think so?"

Wendy thought he could seal the deal if he paid for her damn Lexus to be towed. She preferred to stay quiet on the matter.

A thick, rubbery sound squeezed through the air as a car spun its wheels on the blacktop. The rain had turned it into oil. Through the dripping windows, Wendy watched Kerri run back with a newspaper over her head. When she got back in, her hair was wet and

69

her makeup had run a little (*like she's melting, ha-ha!*).

"Well?" Andy asked.

"They say it's gonna take two hours."

"What?"

"Yeah, they got a lot of calls. But you know what? It's cool. I'll just call a cab or something. I'm sure they'll –"

"I won't hear of it," Andy said, palms up. "I'll drive you."

She looked at Wendy. "But what about –"

"Wendy," she said. "My name is Wendy."

Kerri gave her a lopsided *sorry, I should've remembered* smile.

Andy asked, "You have a problem with that, sweetie?"

There was a long pause in which another thunderclap made an appearance.

"I guess not," she said, and Andy started the car.

It didn't take long to get to Sea Cliff. The closer they got to the Hempstead Harbor the harder the rain fell. Wendy thought back to the incident last summer, with the boys behind Hyde Hills, as Kerri and Andy swapped life stories.

It seemed to her that Kerri hadn't done an awful lot. She'd been an actress almost all her life, while waiting tables and working at the local multiplex. She wondered why women trying to get into this profession always took menial jobs and she figured it was because they had to watch people, get the measure of them, so they could recall their habits and conversation when auditioning for a part. That's what Kerri was doing now: trying out for the role of Andy's new girlfriend. Wendy knew it was a bad idea, which is why she reverted back to the powerful memory, the one that had frightened her therapist, Dr. Weinstein.

The two boys were in sophomore year, high school. She wasn't afraid of them. They always seemed to hang out behind her school, and once or twice the cops were called to assess their damage. They liked to blow things up. It was what they did for fun. It started, she knew, with a small box of lighter fluid. They found a spot in the gully behind the soccer field where a giant oak climbed toward the clouds. They liked to squirt patterns onto the bark and light it with a thrown match. One of them burned his arm once. They didn't come back for a while after that.

According to one of her teachers, the boys had been arrested for obtaining illegal fireworks. They were the kind of things you could get everywhere around July 4th, which had been a week away at the time. Wendy heard them scuffling in the bushes when school let out (she'd listen for them), but after a while, there was nothing, not even the breeze that so often whispered through the crab-grass. It came as a surprise when she heard the sonic whistle of projectiles soaring through the air, followed by a luscious *bang* that seemed to signal the first strains of war. This had been a day when she'd suffered the wrath of Miss Patterson, her cranky math teacher (*stupid bitch, wish she'd leave me alone*), and when the corner came that would take her to the school bus, she strafed into the bushes and followed through the ferns until the two boys were in sight, laughing like hyenas, with hands black from handling fire. It was enough to make her develop a sexual curiosity for them.

"What's with the little whore?" One of them said.

Out of the two, the boy with the scarecrow arms was the least aggressive (the fat one didn't know when

71

I Bleed, Dead!

to keep his mouth shut).

"What do you want?" the skinny boy asked.

Wendy shrugged. She felt a little foolish in her flannel skirt and peasant blouse. This wasn't an occasion when looking darling would work.

"You got bottle rockets or something?"

"Yeah," the fat one said. "And what of it?"

The skinny one looked her over, made an assessment, then pulled a fresh firework from behind his back. She figured he'd had it trapped in his jeans.

"You want to light one?" he asked.

She smiled (*ka-boom!*) and reached for it. It was red and purple, with a black wrapper glued to its base. The head looked hot and mad.

"Got a match?" she asked.

"Sure, darling," the scarecrow said. "You wanna use my Zippo?"

The fat one howled, like he'd said something dirty. Wendy was just concerned with the fire, with the smell of gunpowder, already dispensed, that peppered the air. Looking for a good place to set it off, she realized the ground was littered with huge chunks of white foam and fur. She was about to ask what it was when the skinny boy offered an answer.

"We've been blowing up stuff. That was Frankie's old teddy-muffin."

The fat boy, obviously Frankie, grinned and jigged a little, like he'd been shot with electric current.

"You got anything I can blow up?" Wendy asked.

There was movement in the corner of her eye, something fast darting through the grass. A plane flew overhead, scoring the high blue with a white streak. The scarecrow made a quick left, then a right, and suddenly dived head first into the bushes, his arms fly-

With This Ring.

ing in all directions, while Frankie ran forward, excitement climbing his features until he was near hysteria.

Wendy was startled by their sudden movement, but not scared. Traffic sounds came to her, the city moving away from them.

"Hold still, you little runt!" one of the boys said (she couldn't tell which), and a moment later, there was a supreme moment of violence as Frankie brought down his boot, time and again, on the creature the scarecrow had caught in his hands. The scarecrow picked it up, slammed it against the hard earth, and then laughed as he caught his breath, the sound ricocheting through the trees.

"How about this, little miss?" Frankie asked. Dangling from the scarecrow's hand was a dead bunny rabbit.

Wendy thought about this. She felt a sick compulsion to run (*the teddy was blown to a thousand pieces, think of the mess, it won't be pretty – boom! – nosirree*), then she reconsidered. There was no one around, the place was empty. The two boys were standing there, almost regal in their stance, with the innocence they had just killed, helplessly, as a prop in their after school activity. The way it hung there, twitching now and then, reminded her of a pork chop Andy had offered once to their neighbor's dog, Chester. It had the same meaningless quality.

When she made up her mind with a cold nod, the boys pulled the creature's legs apart. Wendy and her two friends inserted the rockets, one at a time until they pushed against bone, then she grabbed the Zippo (*watch it fly!*) and lit the fuse. They all ran to the bushes. About five seconds later, it rained blood.

73

| Bleed, Dead!

Back in the BMW, Wendy twisted the head of the doll, watching the rain as it slid down the window. Finally, they came to a stop outside an apartment building in Sea Cliff, the sky a tremendous black. As a *thank you* gesture, Wendy asked Andy in for a cup of coffee (she said she had some hot chocolate in the kitchen for Wendy). Andy couldn't resist, even though he rarely drank the stuff (his heart was in bad enough shape as it was).

They made their way up to the apartment, running to avoid the rain.

A month later, it was a lock. Andy and Kerri were having a great time. It was a good story, too, and Andy always thought lasting couples had good meeting stories. In fact, he told it to his staff regularly at the restaurant. He treated Kerri to the finest meals, luxurious gifts. Jewelry, flowers, a surprise weekend in the Hamptons. It was magic. But Wendy knew what was going on here. Someone like Kerri couldn't be interested in her father for what he had to offer, not physically. He was a large man, a beastly man. No, it was his bank account she was after, his prestige in the restaurant business – his assets, to put it lightly.

Wendy thought often about the rockets and how they blew that poor creature into a thousand steaming pieces. She wondered what Kerri would look like with those things shoved up her ass and laughed. It seemed very real to her.

One day, when they had come back from a hot rod show in Westbury, Andy told her they had some exciting news.

"We're going to get married," he said.

Wendy's heart sank. "Really?"

Kerri didn't see her disappointment. "Isn't it won-

With This Ring,

derful?"

"But you guys just met."

It had been three months. It seemed shorter.

"I know it's fast," Andy said. "But we really love each other."

Kerri squeezed his paunch. "It's just meant to be."

The sight was both sickening and confusing. Wendy held her doll, twisting the head until it popped right off. There was nothing she could do.

"Aren't you going to congratulate us?" Kerri asked.

Wendy smiled. It felt evil. "You're very lucky."

Kerri brought her shoulders close to her chin. Her eyes were happy slits.

"I know!" she said.

The date was set for August. Wendy tried to think of some way to stop it. She wanted it back to how it was, just the two of them, father and daughter, their home-cooked meals, the evenings spent together after soccer practice. She was determined to bring those days back (*the Lexus hussy needs to take a bow*).

The first incident that incited her plot to eradicate Kerri, came a day or two after the engagement. Andy was working late, so he'd asked Kerri to make Wendy something for dinner (she was living in Oyster Bay now, in the house they had shared since Wendy's early childhood). Wendy had gotten off the school bus at four and yet Kerri was nowhere to be seen. There was a can of macaroni and cheese in the pantry, and she ate that, cold out of the can, while waiting for Kerri to show. Finally, at nine pm, just an hour before Andy was set to return, she heard a car pull into the driveway. When Wendy peered through drapes, she saw a red Taurus with a young man at the wheel. He looked fresh out of college. Wendy watched for a moment,

I Bleed, Dead!

then, as she was about to close the drapes, she saw Kerri's head rise from his lap, carrying a smile with it as she wiped her lips. It was too dark to see more. But there was no mistaking the scene she had witnessed. She kissed the man on the cheek and sauntered out of the car with the gait of a stranger.

Wendy hid as the key turned in the lock. She ran to the kitchen and began studying the nutritional charts of a cereal box. Kerri threw her keys against the table, eyed Wendy for a second, and sat down to pour a bowl.

"I'm famished," she said. "You want some?"

Wendy shook her head. There was a small pain in her chest.

The second incident came a week later, when she caught an early bus home from school, sick to her stomach with a virus that had inflicted some of the weaker kids. She used the key Andy told her was *for emergencies only* and climbed into the house. There was immediate scuttling upstairs, the work of some rambunctious raccoon, and then a humongous *thump* as if a potato-sack had dropped from the clouds. Wendy had begun to climb the stair risers when Kerri appeared at the top, a towel around her svelte body, even though her hair was dry and there was no steam from the shower. It took her a while to fix her face into something that looked normal.

"Hey, hon," she said. "Whhh-what you doing home from school?"

"I'm sick," she said, throwing down her backpack. "Need fluid."

"Well, I'll… You want some cocoa?"

Wendy nodded. As she looked toward the kitchen, there was a flash of brown in the backyard, and through the window she saw a bald, chubby man, run-

With This Ring,

ning bare-chested with a shirt flying over his back, hobbling with one canvass shoe, into the neighbor's yard and then to the street. Kerri's presence at the top of the stairs did nothing to wipe the image from Wendy's brain. It was what she had hoped for all along, coming to life, like a monster stitched of all her dreams.

It was the final incident that did it.

This came a week before the wedding. Kerri had talked about nothing else except the huge surprise she'd got for Andy, a wedding gift that would blow his mind. Wendy had been sneaking around at this point, trying to find new evidence to secure her knowledge that Kerri was in fact sleeping with anything that moved, except for Andy, who she said could wait until their wedding night. This was a pathetic promise and maybe her father knew it. Wendy knew this bitch had to go, and by golly, she had it coming to her. The gift, she'd discovered through a number of phone calls, was a vintage white Cadillac, which Kerri would drive around the church and pick Andy up in, so they could ride off together toward their piece of paradise. It wasn't all that original, but Kerri seemed to like it. Wendy wondered how she could afford such a luxury and then remembered with whom she was dealing; this broad would take a dime from a beggar, even one who tossed them like manhole covers. Andy didn't see her steal like she did, or if he knew, he never called her on it. He was in love. The fat chef was going to marry and this time it was for keeps.

The week before, there were a lot of arrangements still left undone. Our Lady's Perpetual Sorrow was the church, the flowers were lilies and snapdragons, and the organist would score the scene with 'Jesu – Joy Of

77

Man's Desiring' as the happy couple walked down the aisle (*and then BANG it all goes, back to the drawing board*).

Kerri was talking to someone on the landline real late, and it woke Wendy from a shattered dream in which she was chasing a rabbit down into a hole where tunnels spread out in all directions, dripping with a putrid black ooze. She slipped downstairs in her night dress, the refrains of some old Hilary Duff melody playing in her head, and saw Kerri huddled against the couch, her back to the risers, talking in an urgent voice. Wendy had to struggle to hear it.

"I know, it's just… I understand that, but you can't… Dean, I have to, okay? I can't back out of this now…"

Wendy felt a cold hand touch her heart.

"The church is booked," Kerri went on, all hushed tones. "We have guests and…well, why are you telling me this now, huh? I thought you didn't want anything to do… I'm getting married in six days, does that mean nothing to you? Oh, sure, that's your answer to everything, isn't it? What, are you gonna threaten me now? Andy? He's done nothing to you! Dean, I swear it, if you touch…Dean?"

She must've seen Wendy's reflection in the black glass eye of the television set, because she snapped her head toward her, so quick Wendy almost heard the veins in her neck crack.

"I gotta go," she told Dean, and clicked off the phone. "What did you hear, Wendy? You been listening long?"

"I came down for a glass of milk," she said, as calmly as she could. Kerri moved closer to her on the stairs, her bottom lip pulled down, like a scowling mutt.

"Come down here a minute."

"No thanks."

"Are you defying me?"

She thought about that. The room had gone silent.

"No. I just don't wanna come down there."

Kerri approached her on the stairs, her movements slow and dangerous, like a viper. Suddenly, her eyes were black and all-seeing.

"Do you love me, Wendy? Hmm? Am I your new mommy?"

"I guess so."

"Then you wouldn't want to…*ruin* anything, would you?"

"Nope."

"Good. Then please, let me explain something to you."

Foolishly, she went down to her, freeing up the space so Kerri's arm could snatch forward and grab her neck, squeezing tight, like she was a bottle of shampoo.

"You won't repeat anything you heard to your father, will you, sweetie?"

Wendy met her eyes (*think of the rockets - a million Kerri pieces!*).

"Because Andy, he works so hard for this family. He doesn't need to know I have other arrangements, does he? It would just crush him."

"You don't…love him," she croaked out.

"In my own way," Kerri said, and squeezed a little more. "But your father, he isn't really what I'm looking for in a lover. I need someone who can press my buttons. Andy, well, he can look after me. Can make life worth living."

"You're going to hurt him," Wendy said (*kaboom!*).

Kerri's face was reflective. "Not if you let this go."

Slowly, Wendy nodded. And Kerri eased up the pressure. When she dropped her to the final step, Kerri folded her arms. Wendy could feel the welt on her neck pulsating. Her heartbeat was in there.

"You forget about this little thing and we'll have a good time Saturday, huh? Just the three of us. A real good time."

Wendy nodded again.

"Now, how about that glass of milk?" Kerri asked, and waltzed, like nothing had happened, toward the kitchen.

In the days following, Wendy devised a plan.

It wasn't all that crazy, considering what she had done with the boys. But she knew where they lived, where they kept their stash. A quick visit, an exchange of bills (it was the only time she had stolen from her father – but needs must in situations like this), and she had her solution. After what seemed like an eternity, the big day came, and it rolled on smoothly, like a thrown rug.

All who turned out for the ceremony looked subtle and understated compared to the bride. Kerri wore her dress like it was a second skin, and she knew how to walk in heels without appearing clumsy or gauche. The way she stood, arm linked with Andy at the altar, made Wendy feel they were saying their goodbyes, so somber was the moment, and in a way, that pleased her (*hell yes, can't wait for her to start that car, my God, it's just gonna be a riot!*).

Wendy was given the job of handing Andy the ring; something denied the best man (a fellow chef at Kevecki's). When she gave it to him, he smiled and treated her to a wink. The look on Kerri's face was

With This Ring,

pure steel and it made her wince a little.

A few holy words and the service was over. They were married (*hurrah!*) and it was time to head out into the big bad world. But first, Kerri's surprise (*here we go, it's show time – hope I did it right, please, go off without a hitch*). Kerri led Andy by the arm toward the entrance to the church, where the car was clearly visible. Somehow, it had been covered from sight, with a cloth, Wendy figured, because it was there last night, otherwise, how could she have done what needed to be done?

She wondered now, in her adolescent panic, how her father had missed it or how Kerri had left it unguarded when she knew how much it was worth, and how the company she'd used to hire it had let her keep it overnight in an unwatched parking lot, but none of that mattered, because there was a man standing before it now, wielding a baseball bat, looking intently for someone about to meet the end of it. Something dropped in Wendy's stomach when she saw his eyes meet Andy's. There was a moment of hesitation, and then the man came running, holding the bat high above his head, screaming with the feral roar of a black bear.

"Dad?"

But it was too late. Andy had already worked out the remaining seconds of his life. It was written out for him, like a sad eulogy, by Kerri's actions and the events she had set into motion. The gathering parted, the sun winked against the white Caddy's paint job, and with a dreadful flash, the bat came down on Andy's head, again and again, until he went down. For the second time in Wendy's life, it rained blood.

"Dean!" Kerri shouted. "Dean, that's enough!"

I Bleed, Dead!

And yet the man named Dean didn't think so. He continued his thrashing, more violent with every swing, his bitter face twisted in a grimace that reflected the purest of evils. Kerri grabbed his arm and he pushed her back. Someone in the crowd had their cellphone out, calling 911.

When Andy (a sea of blood) could no longer move, Dean ran across the lot, his footsteps leaving crimson prints against the cinder, to the horrified screams of the gathering, family members who had witnessed murder, the Reverend who had seen the black work of the Devil.

Wendy turned to Kerri, who wept like a child suddenly orphaned, and said, "You were supposed to die! Not Daddy! It was you. It was supposed to be YOU!"

Soon the paramedics came and Kerri followed Dean's bloody footprints into the brush, out into the wild. There was nothing that could console the girl, not after such brutal violence. She kept telling them something about bottle rockets and kerosene but none of them knew what she was talking about. The wedding guests hung around to give the cops their statements and then dispersed, traumatized. The sun hung heavy that night and the temperature was the highest of all summer.

Later, as the paramedics were about to take Wendy to St. Blooms Medical Center, a figure in a white blood-flecked dress crept toward the Cadillac that had been a gift for the deceased.

There was a smile on the girl's lips when an explosion rocked the cinder lot and sent fireworks dancing above a spectacular conflagration, into the sharp evening sky.

With This Ring.

The Axe Bride
The Nightmare Jane

Maggie stepped reluctantly from the massive prison that had been her home for the past three years. The air that wandered gently across her face was somehow gentler, more delicate than the air on the inside of the yard. The sky, tempted to rain, foretold the dangers of freedom. Maggie trod down the walkway, feeling the prison walls fall away from her as she moved. It had been three years, and a jury vote of Manslaughter had locked her away in that hell. Away from her family, her only surviving family.

Orphaned young, she had grown up in foster care, clinging to the only brother she had left. Then he too died, as a result of gun violence, while she was on the inside. She had never even seen his grave. With no children, no husband, no parents and no sibling left to comfort her, she was all alone under that trembling sky.

Six years ago she had been wed, in a massive white ceremony in front of all of her friends and family. It was the happiest day of her life. Her new beau showered her with affection and she returned each embrace a hundred fold. But that only lasted a month. Then she began seeing another side of him, an ugly, angry side. At first she didn't know if she was doing something wrong. Maybe inexperience was causing her to make mistake after mistake. Where she put the TV remote, how loudly she put away the dishes, if she left toothpaste on the sink after brushing. Gradually, she began to see that it was not her, but him. But it was too late, when he started to beat her.

She decided to kill him one morning over breakfast, when he slammed her into the kitchen sink. She thought about it for many months, going through the planning stages as if it were just a lovely dream. She thought about how she would do it, if she would buy a gun or use poison. Poison seemed to be the way to go, but she got lost in the pharmacy, and didn't know what might kill a person. Finally, she got cash out at an ATM and purchased an axe at a hardware store. Then she stayed up at night, every night, until he fell asleep, and tiptoed downstairs to look at the axe hidden in the garage. One night he raped her, or forced himself on her without giving her time to say no. She cried and apologized and went to bed beside him. Then she woke herself up early in the morning, crept out to the garage and laid her hands on the axe.

He was still sleeping when she came back in. She raised the weapon high above her shoulder and brought it down with all her strength, right into his head. His body twitched, shaking the bed terribly. Maggie rocked it out and slammed it down again. The horrible specter of death stared back at her, red beneath the shining metal of the axe. She ran, without waiting to see the outcome. She ran all the way to the corner store, in her nightgown, and called the police.

She waited until they came, and shook in disbelief as they took evidence samples from her hands and clothes. Then they booked her and began the trial that would take away her freedom. She had a history of broken bones, fresh bruises and an internal tear that confirmed the rape. But he had not been attacking her when she killed him, he had been asleep. That fact alone earned her the three years from a largely sympa-

With This Ring,

thetic jury.

Maggie blinked in the summer sun and saw a man waiting against an old white Honda, at the edge of the road.

"Maggie Mckelwie?" the man approached her.

"Cunningham." Maggie corrected – her maiden name.

"Hi, I'm David. I knew Bradley." He was her brother, deceased one year now.

"Hi."

"Can I buy you lunch?" David offered, gesturing back toward his car. "You know I saw Bradley right before…and he said that we should all go out, once you got released."

Maggie smiled. "Sure." She would have to hit up the social service agencies for food and a place to stay, but lunch with one of her brother's friends seemed like a good way to stall.

"How did you and Bradley meet?"

"We worked together at Amos Brothers." David went around to open the passenger side door, holding it back for Maggie to step in.

She grinned and shook her head. *Who said chivalry was dead?* She slid into the passenger side seat, wondering at her luck. With no one to go back to and no prospect of a job or a place to live, this man was waiting for her. She wondered briefly if he was telling the truth, if he really knew her brother and was being as courteous as he said he was. So she asked a few questions, just to calm her nerves. What was her brother's favorite band, and did he wear a tie to work. David answered the questions honestly: he didn't know Bradley's favorite band, and no one but the manager at Amos Brothers ever wore a tie. It was a meat packing facility, one that Bradley had worked at since he got out of high school. The answers soothed Maggie's nerves, and she set her head back, content to let this stranger take her out to lunch.

He took her to a local diner and paid for her order of a Gyro with fries. They talked about Bradley and about movies they had seen, actors that they liked, old TV shows and mimicked the karate yells found in some of the old Jackie Chan films. She thought he was funny, and appreciated him not bringing up her husband or her time in prison. She would talk about that later. Right now it was important to be normal and alive, out in the world that had shunned her for too long.

"Do you have a place to stay?" David asked, as they stared at each other after paying the check, reluctant to leave.

"Oh, I have to see if I can get into a shelter." Maggie responded, dreading the task.

"Let me get you a room. At least for a week." David reached out to touch her hand across the table.

Maggie pulled away. "It's not like that."

"No, no." He blushed, turning an adorable shade of red, "I mean, just for you. To help you get on your feet."

"Really?" Maggie frowned, confused. "I couldn't pay you for it."

"Well, maybe you would let me take you out to lunch again?" He was obviously interested, but doing his best not to make it a sex-for-favors situation.

Maggie decided she could stand to have lunch with him again, and she could stand to have a place to sleep for the next week. So she accepted, with a shy smile, and chatted with him as he drove over to a cheap mo-

With This Ring,

tel.

That week turned into two, and David called on her every day. Maggie found that hole in her chest that was forged with an axe, soothed for the first time since that horrible night. If his sinister motive was to become her boyfriend, he succeeded. She eventually moved in with him and found a job at a local fast food restaurant.

Nobody knew her history except David, and she eventually opened up to him. Drinking wine to help herself get through it, she described her ordeal and cried into his arms when he told her he loved her. He said he expected nothing short of the same from her, were he to ever mistreat her in such a fashion. She smiled through her tears, and promised that she would.

Their wedding was in March. Maggie wore white again, and had no friends or family to witness the event. They did it at the justice of the peace, in an office with an official witness. David made some joke in poor taste about signing his own death certificate. Maggie put it down to nerves. David had never been married; she was the veteran, such as it was. And despite all of the horrors of her first marriage, she was determined to make a better life with her newfound best friend. Once they had signed the papers, they drove home to their tiny apartment, in love and newlywed.

"Maggie," David lit a candle, using that candle to light five others. They were sharing a salmon dinner, too poor and nervous to go on a honeymoon vacation.

"Yes?" She felt like she could melt away, completely blissed out with this, her second husband.

"I have something to confess."

I Bleed, Dead!

She sat bolt upright. All stray nerves in her stomach tightened, burning and humming in anticipation. This couldn't be good, whatever he had to say. She didn't know how she knew; it was just by the tone of his voice and the way he held himself when he said that, too carefully, too delicately.

"I didn't know Bradley." He put the lighter down, gazing at her intently across the open flame. "I killed him."

"What?" Maggie lost all her breath. She didn't even understand the words that her love had spoken. What did he mean? Surely he didn't mean that he had actually killed her brother? Not in the same way that she had killed her husband. Not in this life. Not her David.

"What?" She whispered, fearfully.

"I killed him Maggie. I love you so much, I did it for us."

She couldn't seem to say anything. This didn't make sense.

He made a sudden move toward her, grabbed her hands into his own so that the candle flames jumped. "When you killed my brother, I never wanted revenge."

"Your *brother*?" The world was spinning in her eyes, the floor rocking gently beneath her feet.

"My brother," David confessed, squeezing her clasped hands reassuringly. "My older brother, he was always a brute. He beat me when we were children. He locked me in an attic for five hours, he killed my dog when it was just a puppy. I never met you because I didn't want to know him, I didn't care. I left home as soon as I could, and never looked back. When I heard he had been murdered, I came to see your trial. I had

With This Ring,

to know the woman who had ended his reign of terror. I know what you endured with him, I felt it; it was the same for me too. I fell in love with you then, a long time ago Maggie."

"But why did you…?" She couldn't even say it, couldn't put name to the nameless fear that was growing drunkenly inside her.

"I had to Maggie, don't you see?" His eyes were lit with a weird flame that had nothing to do with romantic candle light. "I had to hurt you the same way you hurt me. Now we're destined to be together. We're bonded."

"No." Maggie shook her head, pulling her hands away from her husband's. Her stomach pitched, and she reeled away, headed for the bathroom. The salmon came up in great chunks into the toilet, as her mind fought to understand what was happening. How could he do this? Betray her this way? Injure her far more than his brother had ever done? Was she destined to be alone? Raped on every level that a human being was capable of? Courted and used, lied to? No. That wasn't going to happen, not today or any day. Maggie stood up, brushed the hair out of her face and washed her mouth out with water. This bastard was going to pay for what he had done to her brother.

She went back into the living room, smiling gently now.

"How could you have known?" she wondered aloud.

"Known what?"

"That our brothers' deaths would bring us closer?"

"I knew from the moment I saw you," he answered, in his sick, confused assurance.

"So what now?" She trailed a soft finger along the

edge of the couch, leaning forward to blow out the candles.

"Now we go about our lives, buy a house, have some babies." He thought she was buying it, and slid close to her to wrap strong arms around her waist.

"Mmm. Babies," She cooed.

Later that week she bought an axe. She would have liked to buy a gun on the street, that would be un-traceable, but she didn't have the contacts for that. She asked one of the kids at work, as innocently as she knew how.

"So, Damon, you know where I can buy a gun?" She was scrubbing the floor and he was peeling pota-toes.

"Naw. That's what got me thrown in jail before," he grinned, lopsided and genuine.

"Oh, well, I wouldn't want to get you in trouble again." And that was the truth. She would get herself in trouble again. Just like her first husband before this. She had a variety of options open to her. She could use poison, but didn't know much about chemistry, and didn't think she could get David to drink a whole bot-tle of rat poison without figuring out what she was up to. No, a gun would be best. She went to the gun shop only to learn that felons couldn't own guns. So she couldn't even buy a gun legally to kill the man who had killed her brother.

She got cash out at an ATM and went to a hard-ware store, a different hardware store. She bought an axe, telling the sales person that there were some bushes in her yard she wanted to cut down. Then she bought some sleeping pills at the pharmacy and took them home with her.

Maggie put on a pleasant face, and withstood the

With This Ring,

affections of her husband once again.

That night she cooked David's favorite soup, and poured it out into two bowls. In his bowl, she emptied the contents of three sleeping pills, enough to put him down and keep him down. He smiled unknowingly, as he slurped the soup, knowing only that she had put in at least an hour of hard work cooking it. Maggie smiled back, sipping her own soup delicately, awaiting the time when she would have her revenge. The axe was still wrapped in its plastic, hidden in the closet.

After supper, David sat down in front of the television, and began to close his eyes. Sleep tugged at him with strong arms, dragging him down and backwards into a darkened abyss. Something felt wrong, the force of the drug was too powerful. David forced his eyes open and stared at his new wife, moving purposefully around, cleaning the apartment.

"What did you do?" he slurred, certain that she had put something in the soup.

"Hmm?" She looked up, as if innocent.

"What did you put in the soup?" He staggered to his feet, still feeling the heavy hands of the drug in his brain.

"Nothing, sweetheart," Maggie smiled sweetly. "Go to sleep."

"I have to get out of here." He lurched to the door, grabbed his keys and his wallet and reached for the door knob.

She pushed him away, swinging her whole body into the action, dumping him drunkenly against the couch. "No." She grunted, getting low to ward him off.

"Out of my way!" Sleep was coming now, like a dark serpent on wings, ready to devour him.

"Never!" she swore. "You killed my brother!"

91

"Ahh." So that was it. He had thought she understood. He had confessed only in the hope that it would bring their love closer together. But she had not understood, no, she was furious. He saw that now, as his legs weakened, as the world began to spin. He held on, desperately trying to fight for his life. It was clear to him what was happening. She was killing him the same way she had killed his brother, she would do it now without a thought for the love that they shared. David hauled back and rammed her into the wall, choking the breath from her lungs.

Maggie cried out in surprise. She clawed at her husband's back, pounding on him with fists, though it did little good. David forced his hands around her neck, cutting off her air supply. The drug was slippery behind his eyes, waiting for him like a mist. She was going to kill him, if she hadn't already. He had to get to her first. Together, they slid down the wall. She, searching for a way out of his embrace; he, gradually succumbing to the sleeping pills.

His grip grew lighter and lighter against her windpipe, until suddenly she could breathe, curled up beneath him on the floor. She gasped deep fresh air gratefully, feeling the full weight of her husband's body slumped above her. With a massive push, she rolled him off of her, and sat up. The world spun. That stupid bastard. Maggie hoped there would be visible bruises against her throat, so the cops could take pictures when they came to arrest her again.

Was she really going to do it? A second husband? Another trauma?

David lay awkwardly on the floor, sleeping finally, though possibly not for very long. Maggie clattered to her feet and struggled her way over to the closet.

With This Ring,

There, sitting among the shoes and the coats, was the axe. This time she unwrapped it carefully, her mind spinning.

Flashbacks of that night long ago came back to her. The feel of the axe as it swung through the air, the soft split of the skin as it opened for the weapon. The stick of the thing as she tried to pull it back out and the satisfaction of the downswing when she knew it would be her last. All that came back to her as she left the plastic wrapping on the floor and trudged back to her second husband. The brother of the first, who had killed her own beloved. He deserved to die. She deserved to be the one to kill him.

She lifted the axe high above her head, looking down at his sleeping form beneath her. All she could see was her first husband, lying in bed, his face a hamburger of mashed flesh. The axe trembled in her hands, wanting it so bad. She saw herself striking again and again and just prayed for the strength to do it one time, just one more time, to silence her pounding heart and avenge her brother's honor. But she couldn't do it. Not again.

Maggie sat down, the axe clattering uselessly to the floor beside her, and wept and waited for her husband to wake up.

The Bonds of Love

Danica Green

David woke with his head pounding, eyes closed tightly against the brightness. He could see through veined eyelids. An aching arm reached up to touch his lip, painful and crusted. An experimental lick revealed the metallic taste of blood. He tried to open his eyes and flinched at the orange light, closing them and breathing deeply through a wave of pained nausea that gripped him.

He opened his eyes again, small slits through which he could see a wooden ceiling writhing with mold. He turned his head to the side and was greeted by a mangy dog that licked his face with alacrity, shocking him into some semblance of wakefulness. He sat bolt upright, eyes wide, ignoring the pain that suffused his joints. He sat in a medium sized room with wooden walls and floor, a table to one side covered in a cream cloth and a dozen bright candles. A vase of lilies sat in the center, wilting slightly in the muggy air. The dog panted enthusiastically by his side and David's brow wrinkled in confusion. A bible sat next to the creature and, upon inspection, David found the dog's collar to be a mock-up of the black and white worn by priests. He tried to stand and sat heavily back down, his body un-coordinated and unresponsive. That was when he noticed his own attire. He was clothed in an old tuxedo, many times patched and considerably too short for him in the arms and legs, the bow tie hanging limply and badly, knotted at his throat. A spasm of coughing brought up a clot of bloodied

With this Ring, I Bleed, Dead!

phlegm and as the coughing subsided, he heard a door close on his right and turned his aching neck toward it.

"Hello sleepyhead," said the woman who had entered, grinning broadly and walking over to the table, fiddling with the lilies and picking brown flecks off their petals. "No need to rush, we still have hours." David tried to speak and began to cough again, eyes open, watching the woman gleefully arranging the candles into perfect symmetry. She wore a brand new wedding dress, lustrously white, though the hem had become soiled from the dirt on the wooden floor. Her dark blond hair was held with tarnished silver clasps and the silk gloves that trailed up her forearms were dirtied with a combination of soil, candle wax and blood.

"Who are you?"

The woman laughed sharply, the sound of a braying horse combined with a snort as it cut off abruptly. "I don't want to play your games David. There's too much to do."

"How do you know my name?" He asked with a heavy swallow and another cough.

The woman glared him to silence and finished her arrangements on the table, beaming at the result and stepping back to admire it. "What do you think? I would have liked more flowers but there was so little left in the fund after the dress." She punctuated the point with a twirl and stopped to look in David's direction, smiling.

"I...recognize you from somewhere. What is your name?"

The woman's face dropped into a scowl and she walked forward, slapping David hard around the face. The shock, combined with the aching uselessness of

With This Ring,

his limbs caused him to fall back and sprawl across the floor.

"I said we have too much to do. You need a bath." She stormed from the room and David heard the distinct click of the door being locked behind her. His mind reeled, trying to recall his last memory from before this place, trying to picture the woman's face in his mind and connect her to something, but all he could focus on was the throbbing pain and how weak his body felt. The door clicked again and the woman entered with a large plastic bowl of water and a rag. She knelt beside David and reached out to his face. Still lying on the ground he shuffled away and kicked his legs at her as well as he could.

"Stay still," she ordered in a tone that negated questioning. He continued to writhe and kick, until any energy he had managed to regain was expended and he collapsed back to the floor, immobile.

The woman scooted over and began to wipe the wet rag across his face, making his lip sting as she vigorously scrubbed away the dry blood.

"Now, do you think we should read our own vows or use the generic boring ones? I've jotted a few things down but you'll have to get a move on if you're going to get yours finished in time. I wouldn't mind - *hold still* - using the generic ones though, the end result is the same of course..." She giggled and continued to talk in an unstoppable stream, cleaning and re-wetting the cloth until the water in the bowl was a dirty pink.

"Carla?" The word came as a croak from David's mouth as the shock of recognition hit him.

"Yes?" she smiled, continuing her ministrations.

"What...I haven't seen you in ten years."

"Hmm? What? Oh never mind, no time for idle

chitchat. I have to go and do my make-up. You stay and talk to Father Rufus about the ceremony. I want to make sure everything is perfect." She gestured across the room at 'Father Rufus' before leaving and firmly closing the door. David turned his head to see the strangely attired dog cocking a leg to piss up the side of the table.

"Rufus," he whispered, and the dog bounded over to lick his cheek, then yawned and dropped to the floor beside him. David rubbed the dog's shoulder and summoned the strength to prop himself against the wall, head lolling on the end of a flaccid neck.

He and Carla had been at school together, she in the grade below and making no secret of her attraction to him. He'd mostly ignored her, but after the summer of her penultimate year and his last, she had come back to school as a busty, silken haired goddess, a complete contrast to the dull, quiet, unwashed stick she had been before. Her attentions still held fast to David and he'd had no qualms with taking her as a girlfriend, a hazily remembered excess of sex and cocaine. She had always been clingy, disgustingly possessive but he'd been an eighteen year old miscreant and didn't care for much besides indulging in her body. When he left for college, he broke up with her and she spent nights outside his house screaming, until the day he finally drove away with her chasing the car down the street, tears in her eyes. There had been rumors that came to him from friends still in the town that she had killed herself. That she had killed someone else. He'd laughed it off and tried to forget her.

Carla returned to the room and crouched beside David. He paled slightly to see a myriad of colors smeared across her face, bright lipstick on her front teeth and blobs of mascara sticking to loose hairs. She held a notepad and pen in her hands.

"What should we serve at the reception? Sausage is a good all-rounder I think, everyone likes sausage."

"We broke up Carla. We broke up years ago."

"Silly goose, if that were true we wouldn't be getting married."

"We're *not* getting married."

Carla erupted into her loud and sudden laugh, punching him playfully in the shoulder, though it hurt more than it should have.

"Sausage then. I was thinking asparagus and cauliflower for the side, maybe cheese sauce, though that can be quite fussy to prepare. What do you think?"

"Why am I so weak? Why can't I move?"

"I told you not to overdo the bachelor party. You never listen to me." She continued to scribble in her notebook and David closed his eyes, casting his mind around for some memory of the previous night.

He had a brief flash of drinking, Jerry and Martin laughing opposite him. A quiet bar. Darts. Cards. His boss Tony smoking a fat cigar. The new girl Maria in a low-cut top. A chilled night out with his work colleagues. He remembered feeling drunker than he should. He remembered feeling sick and embarrassed. He remembered stumbling outside to puke, and then blackness.

"You drugged my drink, didn't you? You were there somewhere and you drugged my drink!"

Carla suddenly pulled back her arm and punched him hard in the face, a torrent of blood exploding from his nose and dripping onto his shirt.

"Don't blame me because you can't hold your liquor, idiot."

I Bleed, Dead!

"They'll notice that I'm gone, they'll worry that I got home safe, they'll call round if I don't show up for work. Let me leave, please!" The last words were lost in gurgles and vomit as Carla pulled a stun gun from her cleavage and rammed it into his chest.

"Flan for dessert," she said blandly as she stood, replacing the gun and crossing her arms as she looked down on him. "The ceremony starts in an hour."

She left the room once more and as soon as he heard the key click, David flopped to his stomach and dragged his body painfully across the floor. When he reached the door he spent a minute trying to get to his knees, and when he finally managed it, spent another minute trying to lift a leaden arm to the knob. When his fingers finally held it he twisted and pulled, knowing it wouldn't move but still trying over and over again in the hopes that the ramshackle wood wouldn't hold together. The door was sturdier than it appeared and he dragged himself over to the corner in case Carla returned and the door got him in the face.

His mind buzzed with a thousand things, trying to piece together a logical explanation for what was happening but he forced it down and tried to focus on a means of escape. The room was empty apart from the table, the bible on the floor and the mongrel that wandered from place to place in a joyless waddle. There were no windows. He pressed his ear to the wall and caught the faint sounds of shuffling, likely Carla running about in whatever room was outside this one. He lifted each limb in turn, experimentally, and realized that his strength was slowly returning, but even if Carla was not armed he would still be no match for her in his current state. He forced himself to take regular breaths. *She's crazy,* he thought. *Bat shit crazy. Talk to her. It's all you can do. Talk to her.*

When Carla entered the room again, she saw him slumped in the corner and made a point of locking the door from the inside. A small char mark marred one of her silk gloves, meat grease smeared upon the fingertips and she crouched by the dog with a hairbrush, gently combing his dirty fur with a dreamy smile on her face.

"Carla..." David began, swallowing past the lump in his throat, grappling for something useful to say or do. She looked over to him with unfocused eyes, smile still plastered unwavering on her face.

"Yes sweetheart?"

"Did you...invite anyone to the wedding? Uh, I know my mom would hate to miss it."

"Of course I didn't invite anyone. They didn't approve. Your whore mother never approves of anything." David nodded at her and tried to seem genuine but in truth all he could think was how pleasant his mother had been to Carla during their brief relationship so long ago, having her over for dinner on the weekends, even taking her shopping a few times. Whatever madness lurked within Carla now, it seemed to be creating its own scenarios of the past to account for why none of their mutual acquaintances were there. And why, David figured, she would object if he suggested he might call someone, not that he knew if there was a phone anywhere close to him. The wooden room that held him was certainly not part of a normal house on a normal street, at least.

When the dog had been brushed, though it hadn't made much of a difference to its appearance, Carla led it to the table and opened the bible on the floor where the dog sat patiently, slowly covering Genesis in a

101

I Bleed, Dead!

thick coating of drool. David struggled to crawl over to them and eventually Carla noticed him wobbling on his knees and proceeded to help drag him across the floor to sit shakily in front of Rufus, seating herself opposite him and pulling her gloves tight up her fore-arms.

"I would have preferred to stand but if we must..." A silence descended and David watched as Carla's expression changed from solemnity, to happiness, to flushed modesty as she listened to a litany that only she could hear. A few minutes passed and eventually she pulled out a sheet of paper tucked into her neckline and began to read with tears in her eyes.

"David," she smiled, one hand reaching out to stroke his knee. "When you asked me to marry you it was the happiest day of my life. I know we had our ups and downs, your stupid family and that dirty little whore you work with..." *She must mean Maria,* David thought, "...but I knew we would come through it because we promised to never stop loving each other. You are my soul mate. These last ten years have been nothing but amazing and I look forward to spending the rest of my life with you."

She folded the paper back into her dress and nodded weepily at some unseen applause. Her eyes turned to David with expectation. After a few seconds, anger began to creep in as he sat silently before her. He coughed, smiled, then grabbed the edge of the table to haul himself to his knees, a deep breath, then on to his feet, bent double and aching fiercely but standing above Carla, who sported a look of confusion.

"It's only right that I stand for this," he reasoned, beaming down at her through the pain and exhaustion. Her eyes welled up with fresh tears as she waited for

With This Ring,

his vows.

"Carla... Our time together has been...interesting. You always were a very beautiful woman and that certainly hasn't changed..." Carla's smile split her face in two, "...but there is one thing I find to be different about you since the day we first met in school. You are a thousand times more of a demented bitch than you were then." With that, he forced his arm out across the table and swept the candles violently toward her on the floor. She screamed as they caught hairspray, the fine materials and gauze of her dress and she went up in a fireball, the heat of which David could feel on his cheeks as he slumped back to the floor.

Carla ran into the wall, her screams choked off as the oxygen was burned away from her lips and her orange-wreathed hands fumbled for the door key. David watched the scalding metal object clatter to the ground, followed by Carla as she tried to roll the flames out, but the inferno was too strong and her dress had melted to her skin. It lasted no more than a few minutes and David watched every second, torn between disgust and relief for himself and the situation, hand stroking Rufus gently to comfort himself as much as the dog.

When Carla finally stopped writhing, her blackened body still flaming in the corner and charring the wooden floor, David hauled himself over to the key and picked it up with a strip torn from his shirt. He could still feel the heat of the metal as he opened the lock and pulled the door open to take his first look at the next room. It wasn't very different to the one he had been confined in, the same size, wooden walls and floor, with a small window set at the front which looked out onto trees and daylight. The room itself had several tables and chairs scattered across it, and several small campfires sat in a ring in the middle of the floor, two of them sporting pans which were boiling over with the smell of cooked meat.

David crawled over and turned the fires off, setting the pans on the floor where they were immediately pounced upon by Rufus. The dog's patchy coat and protruding ribs painted the picture of an animal that hadn't been well looked after, so David gave him a pat on the side and let him eat his fill, taking a strip of meat from the second pan before it was all gone. The meat was succulent and fatty, and David found himself eating another strip before letting the hungry dog finish off the remains. A few discarded vegetables sat underneath tables, and David reasoned that this was the reception feast Carla had been planning.

He looked over to the door that led outside, and steeled himself to get to it, before something shining caught his eye to the right. He reached over to pick up the bracelet and turned it over in his hands, delicate silver with a ballet shoes charm hanging from one side and a clover charm hanging from the other. His tired mind wrapped around the familiarity of the object and he reached up to the edge of the table to haul himself to his feet. The first thing he noticed was the slick wetness of the table surface, the coppery smell of blood as his nose came level with the wood. The second thing he noticed were deep brown eyes looking at him from a pale face, glazed over and dull. Her lips were slack and bloody. Her body lay on a different table, on the other side of the room.

"Maria..." David looked at the two pans on the floor, Rufus licking the sides of each with ferocity, and he proceeded to vomit heavily on the floor, slumping

With This Ring,

down to sit in the wet ooze that was nothing more than water and flesh. Vague though the memories of the previous night were, he remembered everyone getting to know Maria, how she had shown them her bracelet and told them it was a gift from her late mother. David punched the floor and screamed angrily. He had barely known the woman, she hadn't deserved this. His fists clenched and he restrained himself from returning to the other room to exact revenge for the innocent woman on Carla's blackened corpse, restrained himself from looking over to where Rufus was still licking up the last remnants of Maria's gravy.

David headed for the door on hands and knees, the stress and disgust bringing the weakness back to his limbs, the pain in his body amplified. He reached up and opened the door, collapsing on the threshold, the fresh air a welcome relief to his tired mind and starved off a portion of the nausea still gripping his stomach. He could see trees all around him. The place he had been held captive appeared to be an old, abandoned shack that Carla must have found for her purposes.

A bird screamed overhead and David flopped over onto his back, letting the cold soothe his wounds. A dog barked in the distance and Rufus ran outside, jumping over David to return the call, the two creatures beginning a growling conversation across the distance. A barely heard voice sternly talked the dog to silence and David's head swam and he breathed deeply and expended the last of his energy in a loud, pained scream that echoed around the forest.

His face turned up in a weak smile as his mind burned out and the last thing he heard before he lapsed into unconsciousness was the sound of voices coming toward him, running through the trees.

I Bleed, Dead!

Till Death

Christopher Beck

One

Huh? Who goes there? What do you want? Can't you see I'm trying to nap under this tree here? Speak up will you, my hearing ain't what it used to be.

Oh, I see. Come looking for a story have you? Well, who sent ya? How do you know I have some to tell? Hmmm… he did, did he? Yea, yea, I know him. We go way back, me and him. Tell you any of his stories, did he? I bet he did. What did you think of them?

HA! Yes he does.

Well, seeing as he sent you and you done got me awake, take a seat and I tell you one. Only a short one, mind you, for I am but an old man and need my nap.

Two

It's a beautiful autumn day. The sun is sitting proudly up in the clear blue sky. The humidity is low, the temperature moderate. The breeze feels like gentle kisses upon the skin. It is a picture perfect day if you will and a most joyous one for William Sutton.

The big, wide smile on Will's young, handsome face has nothing to do with the weather, however; he could care less about what the day is like. No, my dear friend, I'm afraid that it is something ugly that has Will smiling on this gorgeous day.

The clock set into the dash of his old, beat up, pickup, reads 10:21am as he pulls into the Creek Side Cem-

107

With this Ring, I Bleed, Dead!

etery. It has been a year to the date since William has last been here but he knows exactly where his wife's grave is.

As Will makes his way to his wife's final resting spot, he drains the rest of the beer out of the can he is holding, tosses it out the window, and grabs another from the cooler sitting on the seat next to him. It hisses as he pops the top. He wastes no time in gulping half of it down.

"Hard to believe it has been a year already," he says to himself.

Time can be crafty with the ways that it gets away from you. Indeed, it had been a year since his wife, Tonya, was laid to rest.

"Yup," Will said, still speaking aloud to no one but himself. "It has been a year since I've been rid of that fucking bitch."

Nearing his destination, Will parks his truck in the middle of the narrow road, (fuck anyone who may want to get by) drains the rest of his beer in one long pull, tosses the can, grabs his red and white Cool-Mate mistress off of the seat and gets out.

He can see Tonya's grave from where he is standing, it's not far. The walk up the small hill to it should take no more than thirty of forty seconds, which is more than enough time for Will to relive the night he murdered his wife.

Three

Tonya held the shower head firmly between her thighs while she used her hands to rub her breasts and tease her nipples. The streams of hot water felt good as they massaged her vagina. Her light cocoa skin was covered in gooseflesh.

Will was out drinking with the boys, again, (something that had been a once a week thing, but was now becoming a three night a week thing) so Tonya let herself go, let her primal side take over and let her sighs and moans grow as loud as they wanted to.

Her first orgasm came fast and hard leaving Tonya feel as if an earthquake had occurred within her body. It felt good. It felt damn good, and she was reminded of a time when Will would make her feel this way.

"No," she whispered to herself. "Do not let that ass ruin this for you. Don't think about him; put him out of your mind. This is your time, enjoy it."

There was a time when Tonya would have never been able to push any thoughts of Will out of her mind. Hell, there was a time when she didn't want to think of anything else but Will and their future together. It had only been eighteen months since they married but oh, how times had changed.

She began to work on her second orgasm. Using her fingers in tandem with the showerhead for this one, Tonya took her time. She worked herself close to climax, stopped, and then worked herself close again. She did this until it became unbearable, until she could take it no more. She called out the Lord's name as she let herself go. Her body trembled uncontrollably. Her legs became rubber, threatening to give out on her. Gasping, Tonya let the showerhead fall down into the tub as her back met the wall. Eyes closed, she slowly slid down into the tub next to it.

"Having fun in there?"

Tonya jumped, her eyes flew open and her heart nearly seized up. She looked up and saw Will peering down at her from over top of the curtain rod.

I Bleed, Dead!

"Jesus, Will. You scared the living shit out of me, you ass. How long have you been there?"

Will smiled down at Tonya, it wasn't a nice one, and said, "Long enough to see that I have been replaced."

They stared at each other for a moment before Will stepped down off the toilet and flung the shower curtain open. He studied Tonya's frightened face before turning his attention to the showerhead.

"So, you like this thing better than me?" he asked, while bending over to pick up the fallen showerhead.

Now that he was closer, Tonya could smell alcohol weighing heavily on his breath.

"Will, I…" her response was cut off as Will took the showerhead and sprayed her in the face with it.

Coughing, Tonya turned her face away. "Fucking asshole, what's your problem?"

Will, turned the showerhead so that it was spraying the wall. "Well," he said, his voice smooth, the same wicked smile upon his face, "I asked you a question. Normally when someone asks you a question they expect an answer."

"I was trying to answer but you sprayed me in the face!" Tonya's voice was nowhere near as smooth as Wills.

"No bitch, what you were trying to do was give me an excuse. Now, if you don't want your new boyfriend here crammed down your goddamn throat, I suggest you cut the bullshit and answer me." He shook the showerhead violently in her direction. "Do you, like this, better than, me?"

Never before had Will spoken to Tonya with such venom, not that his words to her were always the nicest but, until this night, they had never been so angry, so hateful, so violent.

"What the hell is wrong with you, you drunk ass-hole?" Tears filled Tonya's eyes as she screamed at Will.

"Me? What the hell is wrong with me?" Will's voice was starting to lose its smooth edge. "What the hell is wrong with you, Tonya? I mean, I'm not the one in here getting it on with the goddamn shower-head."

"No, you're not. But, if you were here with me more often, like you are supposed to be, if you weren't out drinking with the boys all the time, I wouldn't have to resort to getting off with a showerhead." She paused, wiped tears from her eyes and let out a brief, disgusted laugh. "You know what? Even if you were here more often, it wouldn't matter."

"What the fuck you mean by that?"

"Nothing, Will, just forget it."

"Bullshit. You brought it up, so it's obviously something on your mind. Why stop now? You want to say it? Fucking say it."

Tonya took a breath, a deep one. Her heart was a race horse within her chest. Her nerves were fried and her body trembled. She had known for some time now that, sooner or later, this moment would come. Only, she didn't think it would be like this. She looked up into to Will's eyes. They were not the eyes of the man she had married.

"Before we got married," she said, "things were different; you were different. You used to be so sweet and caring. You used to write me poems and hold me close as you read them to me. You used to join me in the shower and gently wash me. You use to tell me, nearly everyday, that I was beautiful. You use to make me feel so special and loved. Things were so good then. But, after our wedding you began to change. The poems stopped, the showers together stopped, you loving me the way you once did stopped, and I don't even know why. You don't ask me how my day was anymore. In fact, anymore, you barely say anything at all to me. The few conversations we do have are all about you. You don't hold my hand anymore. You don't snuggle up to me on the couch anymore. Hell, you don't do anything with me anymore. I mean, when was the last time you took me out to dinner, or a movie? And our sex life, ha, it was good once but that has changed too. You used to make me feel like no other man could. God, it was so good, you were so good. Now you are nothing but a wham-bam-thank-ya-mama kind of guy. It's all about your needs now, to hell with mine. When was the last time you even went down on me? I'm always doing it for you, even though you make it feel like a damn chore." Tonya wiped fresh tears from her eyes, caught her breath and then continued.

"Fuck, Will, you think I like the fact that I have to use a showerhead to get off instead of having my husband do it? Do you think that I like it when on those rare times you are home, it still feels as if you are miles away? Do you think…?"

Tonya could go on no longer. Was there more that she could have said? Yes, lots more, but her point had been made and she couldn't bring herself to go on. It hurt to damn much.

Will, stared at her. It was true, every last word. Part of Will knew this even if he wasn't willing to admit it.

"Yea…well, if you weren't such a needy fucking bitch…"

With This Ring,

"Save it, Will. I love you and part of me will always love you but I can't do this anymore. I just can't."

"What the fuck are you saying?"

"I'm saying that it is over Will. I'm saying that I cannot take it anymore and I am done."

"Done? Done?" Will was now shouting. "Over my dead body. You ain't done, bitch. You're mine. Till death do us part, remember? I will tell you when you are fucking done."

"I'm telling you Will. I. Am. Done. Get it through that thick, drunken skull of yours."

"You think so?" Will's eyes had become daggers. "You really fucking think so?"

"Yes, I…"

Tonya was cut off by Will as he, once again, used the showerhead to spray her in the face. Her eyes clamped shut, and her breath held, as she turned her head away from the water. It was useless, Will followed her movements. She covered her face with her hands. Will slapped them way.

"Better keep them the fuck down," he growled.

With no where to go Tonya cowered into the corner of the shower. Her lungs were beginning to burn. Will moved the showerhead to within inches of her face. The water that had, only minutes ago, brought her to not one but two climaxes, now stung her face.

Blindly, Tonya lashed out. Her open palm caught Will on the bridge of his nose. Pain shot up into his brain. Tears filled his eyes. He dropped the showerhead.

"You fucking bitch. I'll kill you for that."

"Stop it, Will!" Tonya was now in hysterics. "Leave me the fuck alone!" She tried to stand but Will snatched her up by the hair.

"Oh, no," he growled, "you're not going anywhere."

Tonya let loose a yelp.

Their eyes locked. The world around them slowed to a crawl.

Tonya tried to speak, nothing but a hoarse croak came out. She tried to move but was paralyzed.

Will flashed a most wicked and vile smile, one that chilled Tonya to the bone. He bent down so that he was only inches from Tonya's face. He wrapped his hand deeper into her hair and spoke through clenched teeth.

"Till death…"

Time sped back up as Will pulled Tonya's head back and then slammed her face first into the rim of the tub; the sound of which reverberated off of the walls.

The impact knocked out three of Tonya's teeth, broke her jaw, fractured her eye socket and pushed her nose up into her brain. Death was immediate.

Panting, coming down from the rush, Will let go of her hair, stood, and watched as her body slowly slid down into the tub.

"Looks like you got what you wanted after all."

He inspected himself, making sure no blood got on him. Though he could see none, he would still change clothes for good measure. He pushed the bar of soap down into the tub, ripped the curtain off the rod, letting it fall down next to his wife, left the water running, then went into the living room, snatched up the phone and called 911.

He was questioned, more than once, but he remained calm each time and never varied from his story. His night out with the boys gave him a good alibi and, eventually, Tonya's death was ruled accidental.

With This Ring,

Four

Back to the present and our beautiful autumn day.

Will has just reached Tonya's grave. He puts his cooler full of beer on top of her headstone and fishes out a fresh can. As he pops the can open, he surveys the area and sees that he is alone. He takes a pull before looking down at the grave marker.

Tonya Sutton
Beloved Daughter
1979-2010

"Hey bitch." Will lets out a belch and then continues. "Been awhile; how's life treating you these days?"

He giggles at his joke, drains the rest of his beer and tosses the can off into the grass.

"Me? Oh, I've been just dandy since you decided to leave. I can go out when I want. Have a few beers if I want. Come home when I want. And, you know what the best part is? There ain't anybody there waiting to bitch at me as soon as I come in the door."

He belches again. Each word is coming out more slurred than the last. "Oh, hey... I brought you a little something, something. I think you'll like. You wanna know what it is?

"Come on, take a guess.

"Oh, alright I'll tell you.

"You see, I've had about a half dozen beers since I woke this morning and haven't taken a piss yet. Not that I don't need to, because I do. I've just been saving it for you, hunny."

Will lowers his zipper and pulls his penis out. He rests a hand on Tonya's tombstone, leans forward and begins to relieve himself.

"Yea, oh, yea; shit, goddamn, mother fuck that feels good.

"How does it taste, baby?"

Will giggles at himself again and he finishes and shakes the last few drops free.

"Hey," he says, staring down at his penis. "Bet you're wishing now that you never complained about this dick. If you would have just kept your stupid mouth shut, you would still be able to taste this."

He shakes his penis at the ground and it begins to grow within his hand.

"Well, how bout that? He misses you."

A quick look around shows that, besides Will, the cemetery is still empty.

"Hey, how bout I give you another treat? You know, for old time's sake."

He moves forward and begins to rub his penis on the front of Tonya's tombstone.

"Bet you'd like that, wouldn't you, hunny? Sure you would."

Will spits in his hand and begins to stroke himself. It feels good.

"You like that bitch? Like the way that looks? Wish that you could have some of this dick? What would you do if you could? I'll tell you what you'd do. You'd put it in your mouth and suck me dry.

"What's that baby? You want me to get closer? Ok."

Before getting down onto his knees, Will pushes his pants and boxers down to his ankles. He is careful not to kneel in his puddle of piss.

"There ya go, baby, that better?"

The spit in Will's hand begins to dry as he strokes

himself faster. He doesn't care, it still feels good. His body begins to tremble as his climax nears. His eyes roll back into his head.

"Fuck, baby, yea!"

He is on the verge of ejaculating.

"You ready for it, baby? Huh?"

His bicep begins to cramp but he can't stop. He is so close.

"Oh, God…!"

Tonya's partially rotted hand bursts up out of the ground and grabs Will by his scrotum. He screams as her nails dig into his skin. Wide eye, he looks down and can see his blood running down her arm. The ground sucks it up. Even with all the dirt piled on top of her, Will can hear his wife laughing.

He wants to beat the hand away, to get up and run but he can't. Fear and pain has rooted him like a tree. He screams at the top of his lungs but the cemetery is still empty. There is no one around to hear.

With one swift, violent tug, Will's balls are detached from his body. The pain is intense. His eyes tear and nearly bulge out of his skull. He howls so loud that his voice box gives out.

Discarding Will's detached scrotum, Tonya's rotting hand reaches higher and finds his penis.

Five

Well, there ya have it. You came looking for a story and I gave ya one. I told you it wouldn't be a long one but it was still good, no?

I'll tell you what, seeing as how you sat and listened without any questions or interruptions; feel free to come back anytime. I have plenty of stories locked

I Bleed, Dead!

within this old brain of mine; some short, some long. Which I decide to tell to you depends on the day and how I'm feeling.

Well, my eyes are heavy; this old man needs his nap. So, I will bid you a good day.

With This Ring,

Wedding Day Massacre

Jack Horne

Chicago, 1925

It was total pandemonium. Clara screamed and cowered under the table, her wedding dress, bloody and torn. The other guests were also taking cover beneath tables or frantically trying to flee the building.

The gunmen relentlessly sprayed the place with bullets, their Tommy guns almost drowning out the screams. Almost.

Windows smashed. Bullets ricocheted from walls. People caught in the crossfire lay dead or dying. Blood was everywhere, making Antonio's Restaurant seem more like the abattoir his meat had come from.

Clara nervously peered at the blood splattered room from her hiding place. Her husband lay face down in a pool of blood. She wouldn't shed any tears. She knew her father was dead. He'd slumped forward, a huge red hole in his forehead. No tears for him either.

Who would be the new leader: Cousin Ricky? No, he was dead too. Who then? She didn't care. At that moment, all she cared about was escaping the hellhole.

She gasped as a pair of highly polished boots appeared by the table. Trembling, she grabbed a shard of glass. Would she be able to kill the man with it? Her sweating hands couldn't even grip it properly. Should she take her own life instead?

Unable to breathe, she waited. She thought of trying to crawl away. She knew she wasn't injured, but she couldn't move.

With this Ring, I Bleed, Dead!

Slowly, the man lifted the tablecloth.

"George! Thank God!" she sobbed, crawling out and clinging to his legs.

He dropped to his knees, ignoring the blood and splinters of glass on the floor. Holding her as she trembled and wept, he whispered, "It's okay now, baby."

"My father's dead," she said. "They're all dead."

"Yes, they're all dead, darling. The...others...are dead too."

"Jimmy Santana's men," she said and spat.

He nodded. "I'm going to take you away from all this."

"Where?"

"I don't know - anywhere. We'll leave this town and start afresh someplace else." He kissed the top of her dark curls. "Will you have me? I mean, I know I can't offer you the sort of lifestyle you're used to –"

Her dark eyes were red rimmed as she looked up into his face. "I have no life here now."

He'd told her once that his father had been a Sicilian tenor and she suddenly imagined how he'd made the local *signore* swoon, if George had got his looks from him. She wondered why thoughts of George's father had come into her mind at such a time. Perhaps it was because she was looking at the dead singer who'd been entertaining them when the gunmen arrived.

"I'd go anywhere with you," she said.

He kissed her and pulled her to her feet. Hand-in-hand, they crossed the street to his car.

"Let's go now," he said. "Route Sixty Six here we come!"

She giggled and instantly felt guilty. Her father

was dead. Her new husband was dead. Her brothers were dead. Her uncles were dead. Her cousins were dead. George was the only living person whom she loved – but then, hadn't that always been the case?

She spoke her thoughts aloud, as though she needed to confess to someone.

"I…didn't…love…any of them," she said slowly, biting her bottom lip. "Not even my father."

"Maybe you're just numb with shock, baby."

She didn't answer.

"It's okay, anyway. Your father was a hard man to like."

"He was mostly good to me, though –"

"He killed a lot of people." He side eyed her and added, "And he made you marry your cousin Joey. I wasn't good enough, just one of his lackeys."

They drove off in silence.

She felt sleepy. As she snuggled up to him, she remembered their first meeting. It had been nearly a year ago, on her nineteenth birthday. She'd been celebrating at The Bixie Club. George had entered the smoke filled lounge, and looked straight at her. They'd exchanged smiles. His was a guileless grin; hers was sophisticated, she'd hoped. She'd often wondered if he'd known she was Alfie Alagna's daughter. Would he still have been interested? She'd tried to hide her interest when he'd kissed her hand and wished her a Happy Birthday, but her father had noticed. Her father had always noticed everything. "My new man's a handsome boy, but your cousin Joey is for you," he'd said, an unmistakable hint of menace in his voice, his fat face smiling amiably.

Her almost dreamlike state was disturbed by George's sudden expletive. She opened her eyes and

I Bleed, Dead!

saw the concern on his face.

"Sorry I woke you, hon," he said. "We're being tailed."

Gasping, she looked behind them and spotted a car. She recalled her father's constant fear about being followed and knew better than to ask if he was sure.

"Can we lose him?" she asked.

He shrugged. "I'll sure have a go. Hold on tight, baby."

He grinned as he put his foot on the accelerator and they sped away. The car behind also increased its speed. It was definitely following them. Jimmy Santana's men, presumably. He'd lost most of his men that night at Antonio's, but she guessed they wouldn't have all been sent there to the shoot out.

George drove faster and faster. The car behind blatantly chased them.

Clara looked around again and gasped. "It's Jimmy Santana," she said. "I'd recognize that nose anywhere. It's just him and his bodyguard!"

George swore as a bullet grazed the car.

"He wants me," Clara said. "Stop the car and drive off when I get out."

He gave her a reproachful look. "Are you saying you don't intend marrying me after all?" He grinned at her. "Or maybe he's found out I'm a cop."

"What?" She stared at him in fake disbelief. Did he think she hadn't guessed? She wasn't as blind as her father.

Another bullet whizzed by the car. A third hit the door on the driver's side.

"Get down," George told Clara. He reached inside his jacket for his gun.

"I can drive," she said, looking up at him from her

crouched position. "I'll drive as you shoot."

Bullets hit the car as they clumsily exchanged seats. Clara felt in control at last.

She slowed down as George aimed at Santana's car. He scored. He and Santana exchanged shots. Their car was peppered and so was Santana's.

"Bullseye!"

George had hit the bearded man in the driving seat. Santana was alone. He'd have to drive and shoot.

A bullet just missed Clara, but she laughed. Nothing seemed real to her anymore. She had passed the point of being scared. It was all just a jaunt. Just like going to the police in the first place.

George cursed as a bullet hit him. Gritting his teeth, he fired. Santana flopped over the steering wheel, dead.

Clara grinned, knowing George must be seeing her in a new light. She was no longer just the beautiful and pampered daughter of a gangster. Then she realized he was wounded.

"Are you okay?" she asked, but George didn't answer. "George?"

Panicking, she stopped the car and checked for a pulse. Her scream would have instantly told any observer that her lover was dead. She had no one. She had nothing.

Finally, Clara knew what being totally in control felt like. It was she who would make the decision now, not her father. She drove the car at top speed, leaving the highway and catapulting the car over a cliff.

The car exploded on impact with the rocky ground and a plume of smoke rose from the lovers' funeral pyre.

It was the end of the Alagna-Santana feud.

I Bleed, Dead!

Mr. and Mrs.

Rhiannon Mills

I wash my hair and blow it dry, while the terry cloth robe I'm wearing hugs all of the deadly curves of my body, a reminder that I'm not a normal person. I'm a weapon and as such, I will be used at my full capacity soon. I smile at the thought of taking out revenge on the one I once loved. He shouldn't have done what he did to me.

Brushing negative thoughts aside, I put on my makeup, careful with the details. Then, I pin my hair up the way he always liked it. John had always said that I looked like a brunette angel with my hair up in a sweep like this. Today, I will add to his angel fantasy by wearing the traditional white gown and keeping myself as light as air.

At this same moment, John is probably bragging to his groomsmen about the things that will take place during the wedding night. I can hear him now in my head. He's probably saying, "I'm gonna give her the what for!" He's famous for using those terms and it irks me beyond the heavens and hell and back again. He's probably saying that he's got a surprise for me, that he's going to put me in a wheelchair from impact. His friends are most likely encouraging this and the fact that they always cheer him on, angers me even more than the fact that John really thinks that I'd ever let him get away with the things that he's done to me.

He doesn't even remember the things that he's done to me, I'd bet. He probably thinks that he's getting away with it because police never picked him up.

With this Ring, I Bleed, Dead!

He probably thinks that the story will die with him, but it won't. Once he's gone, I'm going to sing like a bird and opt for the insanity plea. I'll get off with a slap on the wrist and then my life will finally begin as a woman free of conviction and full of promise. I'll relocate and change my name if I have to, but this is how it has to be.

For a moment, I think about the good times John and I have had. Those days were the only ones that have slowed things down so far. Times when John would sing to me. Times when he would talk about children we would have, and times that he would bring me breakfast in bed, because I was so sick that I couldn't move, much less cook and prepare a quick bowl of oatmeal or a sliver of toast.

Simpler gestures that he'd made over the last ten months of courtship also showed that he was at least part human being. Gestures such as moving my hair from out my way when I wasn't paying attention were the very threads that held me with him for so long. I don't know how the task at hand got so far shoved out of the way sometimes, but when a woman like me has gone so long without human affection and love, it's easy to be thwarted.

I blink back a tear and remind myself that someone with such a careless nature has to be taken care of before he hurts someone else and possibly kills them this time. I was lucky that ten years of therapy, both physical and mental, was the only thing I required. I could have wound up in a casket instead. John walked away just fine. His wealthy parents and their lawyers made sure that John got community service and AA meetings on the regular as punishment for damn near killing someone else.

With This Ring,

They didn't even follow up to check on me, the helpless victim. They didn't care that I had to live as a vegetable for several months, undergo countless treatments, learn to walk and talk again, see a therapist twice a week for the nightmares that I had, screw a plastic surgeon to pay for scar removal and a whole new nose, and come to terms with the loss of ability to see correctly out of my right eye because a glass shard went straight through it.

John never made the connection, though. My eye, though somewhat foggy looking and a slight shade different than the color of my other eye, he said was just one more thing he loves about me. He created the plastic monster that I am and then fell in love with his creation. Poetic justice doesn't seem to apply to what I'm doing.

I prefer to call it a divine intervention.

I pull my hose on and shake my breasts into the strapless bra that I'm forced to wear so that my dress fits just right over it. Then I pull on a white garter belt and slide my small feet into the white heels that I hate beyond measure. Then, I eyeball myself in the tall mirror that sits wedged in the corner of the small basement room below the church. I blink, realizing that everything I wear, all million layers of white crinkly gown and undergarments, will probably be soiled beyond recognition later with John's blood.

Again, I shake the negative thoughts aside as I realize that at this moment, John is still boasting with his groomsmen.

A knock at the door and a slow creaking announces the arrival of my two bridesmaids, Chloe and Sasha. Chloe's dress is deep crimson and is stuck to her body like glue, pushing her small breasts up to her chin, and fits her exactly as she wanted. It gives the illusion of having a figure, which she certainly doesn't. Sasha's dress is a lighter hue, but falls to her ankles and has a slit up to her thigh to show off her shapely legs. Both girls look absolutely perfect.

Chloe is smiling at me as she says, "Are we ready for our lives to change, huh?"

I smile back and shrug. "Gimme some help with that monstrous dress!" We share a quick giggle as Chloe and Sasha pull my gigantic dress out of its bag and off of its hanger. Chloe takes one side of the garment and Sasha the other as they lower it over my head and onto my body. It rests misshaped against my skin, but the three of us shake it into place, pull and tug at each seam until it fits exactly the way the designer intended.

After a round of ooh's and ah's, Sasha zips me into its stiff form and Chloe ties up the bodice in the front.

"Where's the veil?" Chloe asks, turning to Sasha.

Sasha points to a vanity in the corner where a white box sits. "There," she says, "I'll go get it." She clicks her heels across the hard marble floor and returns with a long white veil.

Chloe lifts the contraption from the box and fits it to my head, rearranging a few hairs before she clips it in place. They stand back and I examine myself in the mirror again. The dress is heavy, but I deal with the weight because soon, I'll be taking it off and it won't matter. John won't mind, I assume.

Minutes later, my friend Simon is linking arms with me. My father is not here, so Simon, being my best friend, is taking his place.

Simon smiles at me and then says, "You're going to have such a happy life. This is just the beginning." Ex-

With This Ring,

citement drips from his face and I think to myself that he has no idea how right he is.

I'll miss Simon when I disappear and change my life…

The wedding march plays and Simon walks me down the aisle where I meet up with John in front of a very crowded Baptist church full of our closest friends and his rich family. Simon releases me and wanders to my side of the church where he sits next to his boyfriend and holds his hand. John's side of the church scowls in distaste and it makes me want to slit all of their throats. John's side of the church is staring down their noses at my side and I realize that this is just one more reason why I have to go through with this. I want to make them suffer, too. Not just John.

As John rests his hands with mine for all to see, the pastor goes on and on from the bible and then rolls on about how marriage is a sacred bond only to be broken by death. He asks if anyone has any reason why the two of us should not be joined and at first, I think it might be a possibility that John's mom might open her big ugly mouth, but John's father holds her shoulder and pats her arm and she is quiet. Miserable, but quiet.

Before we can blink, we are married. I am now Mrs. Annabelle Marie Carlton and I am smiling as though it's the happiest day of my life. We hold hands and make our way back down the aisle and outside to be covered in rice, before we crawl into a limousine and are taken away to a fancy Inn by the beach, a place that my new in-laws have paid for as a present.

John is covering me in wet kisses in the limo, but stops when we get to the Inn. It doesn't take us long to check in because John seems to be in a hurry.

I'm starting to feel guilty when we get into an ele-

I Bleed, Dead!

vator and he says to me, "I've been waiting for this day for years," then he pushes a button and adds, "I'm so lucky to have you."

I kiss him, long and deep, before the elevator doors slide open and we make our way down a long hallway before we find room three-twenty-six and unlock the door with a keycard.

John loosens his tie and then just takes it off, flings it onto the top of a dresser as he kicks off his shoes and unbuttons the top button of his shirt. I stare at him and he smiles again.

"So, this is the beginning, right?" he jokes, and I smile and nod.

He makes his way over to me after he's discarded his shirt and blazer. He runs a cool hand over my bare shoulder and then runs his fingertips down the front of my stupid, heavy dress. Goosebumps cover my shoulder and I shudder at his touch.

Can I really go through with this? A flash of a memory slivers into my head and I close my eyes.

I see the glass bursting with impact against my entire face. I see the small car, a birthday present from my parents, smashing into the size of a large loveseat with me folded inside it. I see blood running over both of my eyes and down my disfigured face. I hear a rescue worker curse about the driver of the other car being only eighteen and drunk out of his mind, but totally untouched because his truck was built like a tank.

"Lucky for them," the worker says, "looks like a slow night...only one car to fool with."

I shiver as John tells me that he loves me. He tells me that he can't live without me. He tells me that he wants to kiss every part of me tonight and that I'm so angelic in my dress that I look as though I'd fallen from heaven so that he could have someone to watch over him on a permanent basis. Then he unzips my dress from the back and lets it fall to the floor.

I smile even though I know what I must do. There's no sense in letting a good erection go to waste is there?

"John-," I begin, but he cuts me off.

"Shhh," John says, "Annabelle, just don't speak just yet." He slides his hands over my hips and down my legs as he bends down on his knees to pull off my white hose.

My lips curl into a smirk, and I close my eyes again as he pulls my panties off slowly, kissing parts of me I'd forgotten existed.

I see bright lights, smell antiseptic, and feel tugging. They're removing glass shards from my skin and trying to reattach a bit of one arm, but I don't know it at the time. I think that I've died. Someone, a doctor or a nurse, says, "She'll be dead before morning, but for the family's sake, let's try and get her together a bit." The lights fade and I fade with them for a while.

John kisses my knee, then the other knee and rises to face me. He whirls my panties around on his finger and flings them somewhere else in the room. I don't know where they land, but at that moment I couldn't have cared less. I think to myself that it won't hurt to have one more night of pleasure with John before I send him off. I could use the stress release to clear my head.

* * *

Two hours later, John and I are entangled in silk sheets. He is sleeping soundly next to me, covered in a

131

thin sheen of sweat and whatever else remained as testament to the consummation. The light is low, but I have a lamp at my side still lit and I roll over to tap the shade so that it glows just a tad dimmer. Next to the lamp is a pack of cigarettes and an ashtray. I light one of the cigarettes with a match and toss the lamp into the ashtray as the sheets slink down to my waist from my movements.

I decide that perhaps being naked while I do it won't be such a bad idea. No clothes to burn later. I had planned on slashing him to pieces with a knife I'd packed in my suitcase. There would be a considerable amount of blood from the murder. I sit there naked, filling my lungs with smoke. I think that it might be a bit cleaner if I just pick a pillow and smother him to death instead. It would be easy. I could just pick the pillow up and push it over his face, sit on it so that he can't move, and then it's done.

I weigh my options as John continues to sleep until I've pushed the butt of my cigarette out in the ashtray. I sigh to myself and think about other plans we've made for the honeymoon. Tomorrow we are supposed to hit the beach and show off the lack of tans we have in the hopes of fixing that problem. It sounds nice to me, so I fall asleep at John's side. I'll wait until then to do it. After all, I'll be heading off to Alaska in a few days and a tan wouldn't hurt.

We wake up sometime in the middle of the night. John wakes up first and shakes my shoulder lightly to rouse me with him.

"I'm going to take a shower," he says before disappearing into the bathroom.

I join him. After our shower, we crawl back into bed and he wraps an arm around me while he grabs the

With This Ring,

remote control from his bedside table and flips on the television. About ten minutes into his channel surfing, he stops at a news channel and becomes immediately engrossed in the story.

I sigh out of boredom and begin to rest my eyes, still lying against his shoulder. I fall asleep, but when I wake up he has tied me to the bed by my wrists and ankles. I am still naked but he's covered part of my body with the silk sheet. A gag is over my mouth and I am suddenly somewhat turned on until he walks in, fully dressed in a pair of jeans and tee shirt.

He stares at me. "You are being punished, my love."

I cower.

"You've been a bad, bad girl, Annabelle," he says.

I have no idea what it is he's talking about. Could he have known what I'd planned? It isn't possible.

John paces in front of me and pulls the sheet away. "Did you really think that plastic surgery could cover up the scars? How long did you think it would take for me to realize who you were?"

I tremble. Tears begin to fill my eyes and I watch as he pulls a long blade from my suitcase.

"You were going to beat me to the chase, Annabelle, but it isn't going to work that way," he says as he traces an invisible line from my pinkie toe to my knee. "You thought you were going to take out your revenge on me for nearly killing you, didn't you, Annabelle?"

I shake my head no and blink back more tears.

He pulls my legs apart and stares down at my thighs. "You still have scars, Annabelle, but mine run deeper."

I try to breathe, but my heart is beating so fast that I think it might burst.

I Bleed, Dead!

John traces the blade further down my leg, from my knee to my inner thigh, stopping just where a cluster of odd shaped scars are grouped. "Glass shards stuck there?" he says, then laughs at me.

He laughed at me! My heartbeat speeds up, then slows again as I fill with sudden rage. How on earth can he presume to know what I suffered at his hand?

John runs the blade from my ear to my nose, then down to my lips, but he still doesn't cut me and I wonder what he's waiting for. Is he going to torture me?

He laughs again and says, "Do you really remember that night, Annabelle? Do you remember the people in the car that you hit? Do you remember the passengers in *your* car?"

There were no passengers, I think to myself. I was driving home from the mall alone.

I shake my head no again and this infuriates him. He slugs me and I nearly lose consciousness. Blood spurts out of my mouth from the impact.

"I'll refresh your stupid memory," he says taking a step back, "she was seventeen years old, blond, and perfect in every way. She was going to college in the fall to join me there," he says.

I blink again and for the life of me have no idea what he's talking about.

"Her name was Lizzie and she was whip smart, Annabelle. She was your friend and you betrayed her!" He spat his words angrily in my direction and then ran the blade down the top of my thigh, all the way to my knee, this time cutting me open. "She lost her legs, Annabelle," he says through angry tears.

I gasp through the gag in pain and look down at my leg. Blood spills over onto the sheets and stain them red. I am terrified.

With This Ring,

"Lizzie! Don't you remember her? How could you forget someone like her? She is everything that you aren't, Annabelle!" John is pacing faster and spitting his words at me.

I search my memories. Before the accident, they are foggy and I can't pick her out of anything. Was she a friend? Could this really be true? I don't remember anyone else being with me that night. No one.

"You were drunk," he says, "both of you. But, my Lizzie wasn't stupid enough to drive. Unfortunately, her judgment suffered enough to get into the car with someone she trusted who was also drunk."

I tremble.

"Lizzie and I were engaged," he says, "sure, we were young, but we had big dreams and you took them away from us."

But he was drunk, too, I think to myself. He hit me. I didn't hit him. There was no way I'd gotten it wrong for ten years.

"I looked for you for a few years before I found you," he says, then slices down my other leg.

I scream through the gag, but it only seems to make him happy.

"Your screams are like music," he says, "your screams can't erase hers, but you wouldn't care, would you? You only care about your stupid self!" John then runs the blade straight through my left upper thigh, then pulls it out.

This time my scream is high and shrill. I regret booking an Inn with soundproof walls just then. No one can hear me, just as I thought that if he screamed when I killed him, no one would hear him, either.

"Half of your windshield went through her body. The other half went through yours." John stares at me and wipes the blood from his knife on his jeans. "The shards cut her everywhere. She lost her legs! She was nearly decapitated," he says.

Lizzie, I think. *Who was she?*

"She was going to be a teacher," John continues with his mental torment. "She wanted to teach the special kids because her brother was autistic. How could you take someone so sweet away?"

I blink through more tears and hope to God that John finishes me off or lets me go soon. I can't take much more.

He slices me again, this time running the tip of his blade down one of my arms.

I could have done this better, I suddenly think to myself. John has no creativity. I do not scream this time, but swallow it back instead.

"You took away my future," he reminds me again. "You took away my future wife!"

I shake in my place, but remain emotionless for a moment.

"I never intended to go through with the wedding," he says, "but when we got that life insurance policy, I changed my mind. That was a brilliant idea, Annabelle, even coming from you," he says.

I am somewhat offended, but I just nod. My eyes pool with tears again and this time I can't control it.

He paces. "I don't even know exactly what else to say."

For a moment his eyes lock with mine and I shake my head before lowering my eyes to the seeping gashes on my legs. If I'm lucky I'll bleed to death before he can deliver any more blows.

"I did love you, Annabelle," he stammers, then turns to face me as I look up again. "I loved you so much. But, then I found out who you were. You were the killer I was looking for, but your looks had changed drastically! You whore! You manipulated a surgeon to fix yourself!" He raises his voice and adds, "*Very calculating, aren't you?*"

I am ashamed because I know that this is true.

John reaches into his pocket and pulls out a newspaper clipping that looked as though it had been folded and unfolded a million times before. He clears his throat and begins to read it to me.

"An accident three miles from Mayfield Mall has left one dead and one in intensive care Friday night. The passenger died minutes after impact from wounds received during the accident. The driver, still in critical condition, had been drinking excessively according to police. Services for the seventeen year old, departed, Elizabeth Green, daughter of Dr. and Mrs. Hayworth Green, will be announced tomorrow." John throws the paper down on a dresser and scowls at me.

"Seventeen!" he shouts and I jump, "she was only seventeen."

He shocks me and startles me to full attention now. The blood loss is causing me to nod off, but he has my attention. He jumps on the bed and straddles me with the blade still in one hand.

He pushes it into my chest and it knocks my breath away. The blow was too far to the right to kill me right off, but I'm losing blood fast. He pulls my gag off and throws it across the room.

"What do you have to say for yourself?" he asks me, as though he was asking a child why they didn't pick up their toys.

Our eyes lock. His are bloodshot and I can smell alcohol on his breath. Mine are wide and tear-filled.

"Well?" he demands, spitting through clenched teeth as he speaks.

"I'm so sorry, John," I say, then lick my dry lips, "I didn't know."

He lowers his gaze to my exposed chest and takes my right breast in his hand and then releases it and brings his attention back to my face. I have no idea what he's going to say or how I should respond now, but I am resigning myself to death in my thoughts.

"It's too late to be sorry, Annabelle," he tells me, then shoves the blade into my stomach.

He kisses my cheek and says goodbye, then he climbs over my body and sits next to me, resting his head against the headboard. "You are like an angel, though, Annabelle. I always meant that when I said it, but you're not a sweet one. You're an angel of death because, you see, you took her to her grave and now I'm going to take you to yours."

In my head I wonder just how much more a body can take before its inner light is extinguished and it dies. Can I stand to lose any more blood? I try to hang on to my life.

"John, I'm sorry," I tell him, "but if you just call an ambulance for me, we can put this all-," I stop to cough and sputter blood, "…behind us."

He laughs and turns to face me. "I don't think so. Jail isn't for someone like me. I have a life to live later."

"But, John, I love you!" I say to him.

"You were going to kill me," he says, "that's hardly love."

"You don't love me," I say. He was awfully good at faking that.

"I do love you. In a manner of speaking," he says then adds, "but I loved her more."

With This Ring,

Honestly, that comment hurt, but I look away.

"Annabelle, you can't be my wife," he says, "you're a murderer."

"And if you kill me, you won't be any better," I say, leaning my head to one side. The entire room is spinning.

John chuckles and stares at me. "No, I don't suppose I will be, but I'm doing this for *her*."

I gasp again and shake my head. "Just kill me then, John. I've suffered enough."

He nods in agreement. I expected him to say something, but he doesn't. He drives the knife back into my chest and twists. I watch his unemotional expression as he takes my life. And then, there was nothing.

Meet the Contributors

Jay Faulkner resides in Northern Ireland with his wife, Carole, and their two boys, Mackenzie and Nathaniel. He says that while he is a writer, martial artist, sketcher, and dreamer he's mostly just a husband and father. Jay founded, and edits, 'With Painted Words' – www.withpaintedwords.com - and 'The WiFiles' – www.thewifiles.com – For more information visit - www.jayfaulkner.com

Dorothy Davies is a writer, editor and medium who lives on the Isle of Wight, a small island off the south coast of England. There she writes her strange stories and edits equally strange dark anthologies. She is a full member of the Fictioneers.

Kristian Gore was born in Cleveland, Ohio and grew up in Los Angeles, New York and Virginia Beach. The Navy veteran is currently living in Jacksonville Florida outside city hall as part of the Occupy Jacksonville Wall street protest where he is working on his first full length novel.

Jimalyn Lawless has been writing both poetry and short fiction for ten years but has only been published a few times. You can find more information at http://www.jimalynspot.wordpress.com

Bruce Turnbull started out as a music journalist at the age of twenty. His stories have been published on both sides of the Atlantic, and he has a degree in Creative Writing from Northumbria University, where he edited the campus magazine. He is now working on a full length novel.

The Nightmare Jane has one published book to her name, a historical conspiracy novel titled THE LINCOLN LETTER. She has two children, a husband, two jobs and is going to school to finish up a Bachelors she began long ago. She is not a perfectionist.

Danica Green is a UK-based writer of horribly depressing things, and occasionally things with unicorns in. Her work has recently appeared in such places as Smokelong Quarterly, Neon Magazine, Eclectic Flash and others, as well as anthologies by a number of wonderful publishers.

Christopher Beck, the author of numerous short fiction pieces, some self-published and some traditionally published, lives in Greenwich NJ, where he continues to work on short and long fiction. Follow him on Facebook: http://www.facebook.com/chrifive

Jack Horne married and lives in Plymouth, England, where he works for the local theatre. Quite a few of his short stories, poems and articles have appeared in magazines, anthologies, and webzines, and have also been read out on the radio. He's had some competition success too.

Rhiannon Mills is a stay at home mom and lives in the West Virginia Mountains. With her spare time she has two novels under her belt, a novella, several short stories, and several other projects on their way out to the world. When she isn't writing, you can usually find her either baking or reading.

About the Editors

Charlotte Emma Gledson currently resides in the south-coastal town of Gosport, UK. With over 30 stories and poems published in anthologies and magazines, including articles for the 'The Serial Killer Magazine', Charlotte is also penning a supernatural novel entitled, 'Bluebells for my Baby'. Her collection of unsettling stories, 'The Lonely Tree and Other Twisted Tales of Torment' is available at all good book retailers. Recently Charlotte has been posted poetry editor for Dopamalovi Books. Married with four gregarious children and a collection of ventriloquist dummies and porcelain dolls, she finds time relaxing while sipping wine, singing Karaoke and going on paranormal investigations.

Contact her at charlotte@gledson.co.uk or for more information: www.charlottemmagledson.com

Lyle Perez-Tinics (Writer/Editor/Publisher) is the creator of http://www.UndeadintheHead.com a website dedicated to zombie books and the authors. He is the owner & Editor-in-Chief of Rainstorm Press (www.RainstormPress.com) and The Mad Formatter (www.TheMadFormatter.com) a book interior design business. He has stories in many anthologies and is currently working on two novels, *Existing Dead* and *Rising from the Tempest.* He is the mastermind behind *The Undead That Saved Christmas* charity anthology series. He also writes middle grade chapter books under his pen name, Benny Alano. www.BennyAlano.com

Twitter - @LylePerez @RainstormPress
@UndeadintheHead @Benny Alano
www.Facebook.com/RainstormPress
www.Facebook.com/UndeadintheHead

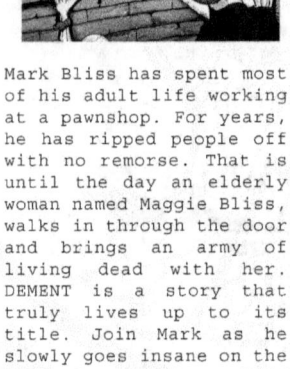
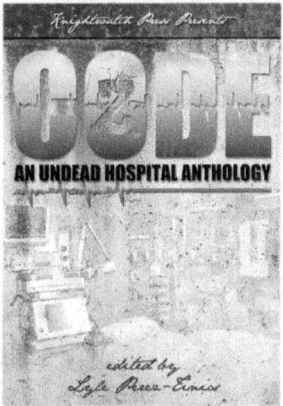

THE UNDEAD THAT SAVED CHRISTMAS VOL. 2

THE UNDEAD THAT SAVED CHRISTMAS VOL 2

Edited By
Lyle Perez-Tinics And Eloise J. Knapp

Another round of ghoulish holiday stories, **The Undead That Saved Christmas Vol. 2** is an anthology of both jolly and frightening proportions. From zombie toys to flesh-eating Santas, Vol. 2 is sure to be the most unique gift under the tree. The Undead That Saved Christmas Vol. 2 brings together various talented authors and artists from across the world.

Stories include: How I Got My Sack Back, by Stephen Johnston; Death and the Magi, by Joe McKinney; Zombies We Have Heard on High, by Jamie Freeman; You Better Watch Out, by Scott Morris, and others.

Get into the Christmas spirit with carols and poems such as 'Twas a Season of Zombies by Rebecca Besser and The Last Noel by Craig W. Chenery.

Whether you buy it for yourself, a friend, or family member, know you're doing it for a good cause. Proceeds from the sales of The Undead That Saved Christmas Vol. 2 benefit the Hugs Foster Family Agency (hugsffa.org) and will help them give their foster children gifts this holiday season. Introduction by Bud Hanzel and John Olson, authors of The Do-it-Yourself Guide to Surviving the Zombie Apocalypse.

Download a free sample at http://www.smashwords.com/books/view/105985

Available on Amazon, Barnes & Noble
eBook available on Amazon's Kindle, B&N's Nook, Smashwords.com

$14.95

ISBN: 978-1-93775-800-4   Library of Congress Control Number: 2011919478

Darkness of Night

a new novel by Mandy Tinics

DARKNESS OF NIGHT
by Mandy Tinics

ISBN/EAN13: 145637768X / 9781456377687
www.CreateSpace.com/3507065

also available at Smashwords.com!

Kaylee's New Year's resolution is to not take life so seriously. As a writer of paranormal romance, she leads a simple and uneventful life. She isn't searching for anything; men are the last thing on her mind. That changes when she locks eyes with a ridiculously handsome stranger. In seconds, her world is turned upside down. Sparks fly, but as quickly as the man approached, he was gone. Kaylee wonders if she will ever see him again. She can't understand how anyone could walk away from something so overwhelming.

Alec, a 253-year-old vampire, has spent years not caring about anyone. His loyalty was to his best friend, Lucian, who was more like a brother than a friend. Darkness of Night is the most popular club in the world. Alec has spent many nights watching humans and even indulges with a few, but he was not ready for what fate had in store for him.

Being half vampire and half human has made life challenging for Alec. He was raised by his human mother, and knew very little about his father. Alec knew he was different because his mother sheltered him from the world. When he looked to be in his early twenties, he finally understood why he was so different.

It is forbidden for humans to know the secret of vampire existence. Now, Alec must choose between losing his true love or jeopardizing Kaylee's life and his existence. In the end will true love conquer all or is it just a line in a book?

Darkness of Night is the debut novel of Mandy Tinics. She is also owner of the vampire book review site, BITE ME at www.Vampires-Bite.com